U0004172

小氣財神
A Christmas Carol
中英雙語典藏版

查爾斯·狄更斯——著　辛一立——譯
亞瑟·拉克姆、彭煥群——繪

晨星出版

導讀

捆綁的人生，微笑的心

文字工作者　董恕明

 故事是這樣開始的

　　老史顧己的合夥人馬利死了。馬利並不是今天才過世，而是一個故去多年的人，雖然他的姓名，始終還被保留在與史顧己合開的店門上。當然，他如果執意要再現身，必定也是個鬼魂之類。

　　至於他的老朋友，那個活著的史顧己先生，「是一個連石頭都能榨出油來的人哪，史顧己啊！是一個用擠、用撈、用刮、用貪、用搵，無論如何都要得到好處的老狐狸！他猶如又硬又尖的打火石，沒有任何鋼棒可以從他身上打出慷慨的火花；而且，他又宛若牡蠣一般神祕、封閉且孤僻」。想想這樣的一個人，他是如何看待這個世界：他曾經快樂嗎？擁有幸福嗎？他會不會爲世人的憂傷感到苦惱？或者他會對自己的處境顧影自憐？

　　顯然這些屬於一般人的喜、怒、哀、樂，早已被他摒棄在外，因爲連在這個最具感恩與歡樂的聖誕佳節到來時，他還是對他生活周遭發生的一切無動於衷。直到他遇見了馬利，一個身後拖著長長鍊條的鬼魂。馬利不理會史顧己的驚恐，他只希望老友不要步上他的後塵：在人世間費盡了一生的心血，結果只是鑄造了一條捆綁住自己的沉重鐵鍊。他告訴史顧己，他會和三位精靈碰面。於是，故事就這樣開始了……。

故事在過去、現在與未來之間流轉

鬼魂來了，精靈也出現了，那些我們一直以爲是存在於想像中的事物，原來並不因爲我們看不見而不存在？就像史顧己見到的三個精靈。他們分別將史顧己先生的過去、現在與未來鋪排在他的眼前，他也因此才終於能憶起，自己在年少時曾有過的正直與歡樂。

只是年輕時的他，寧可放棄心愛的女孩，去追求事業與財富，如今當他垂垂老矣，方才明瞭有再多金錢、再非凡的成就，也填不滿內心的遺憾與失落。精靈帶著史顧己先生重溫逝去的舊夢，是要讓他有機會重新檢視自己過去的決定嗎？畢竟從他下定決心的那一刻起，他往後所走的人生道路，便是完全不同的風景，他把大半生的心力放在事業上，也的確闖出了一點名堂，要不是精靈帶他重歷過往，他還是可以這麼心安理得地過日子，不會覺得此刻的自己有什麼問題。

就因爲這是個特殊的日子，是聖誕前夕，所以他的朋友馬利，才要送給他這樣一個特別的禮物？讓他發現以前他想要擁有的那些東西，實際上並沒有爲他帶來眞正的快樂，就好像現在的精靈讓他看到：職員克勞契先生一家，生活雖然很困窘，卻歡笑四溢；他那個樂天爽朗的外甥，是如何欣喜地與友人迎接聖誕的到來，而他這個舅舅，又是何等愚蠢地拒絕了他熱情的邀約……。

史顧己先生是那麼堅定地從過去走到現在，而他又會迎向一個什麼樣的未來？如果可以讓他重新再作一次選擇，他還會要一個像他現在這樣的人生嗎？

故事該如何結束

英國作家狄更斯（1812～1870）在一八四三年完成《小氣

財神》，廣受好評。相較他的其他著作，不論是自傳性強的《塊肉餘生錄》，或是以法國大革命爲背景的歷史小說《雙城記》，無疑的，這是篇清新討喜的作品。狄更斯筆下的溫暖與嘲諷，在這個故事裡得到了充分的發揮。我們看到一個令人咬牙切齒的史顧己先生，也看到那些雖然生活在貧窮、困苦甚至是悲慘世界裡，仍不放棄喜樂的人。前者的行事作爲讓我們驚懂，但因爲後者的存在，方能令史顧己先生找到人生不同的出口。同時提醒了我們，人的一生，若必須面臨到一連串的選擇，我們在暮年時回頭一望，會期望出現什麼樣的光景？

至少在《小氣財神》中的史顧己先生，最終：「他成了一個好朋友、好老闆、好人，這個古老的倫敦城，或是這個古老世界裡的任何古老城鎮，都知道他是個好人」。是什麼東西使他改變了？我們都曉得他見到了三個精靈，是在一個佳節的前夕。要是史顧己先生始終都沒有這樣的運氣，碰上這一切，他還是繼續理所當然地作他的小氣財神，我們會不會覺得像史顧己先生這樣的人生，其實根本是不值得活的？或者我們要換個角度欣賞，生命即便是會像史顧己先生一樣，但因爲他能獨排眾議，徹底貫徹並實踐自己的信念，所以他無論如何，都還算是個可敬的人？

當然，故事終究會有休止的時候，好比我們的人生。我們在翻開書頁的那一瞬間，也許並不知道這個故事會把我們帶到哪兒去，更遑論那個叫狄更斯的傢伙，又是何方神聖？他爲什麼要寫一個這樣的故事，是不是因爲他想要在這令人不甚滿意的世界，再添加一點希望與光明，就如同上帝爲世人帶來的慈愛與悲憫？

總之，我們是遇見了這麼一個故事，在一路跟著史顧己先生腳步的同時，我們也正走在自己人生的路上，然後不知在何時或是何處，我們也會想起，也能體會——史顧己先生那顆終於會微笑的心。

前言

　　我盡己所能在這本如鬼魅般的小書中，召喚信念的幽靈，希望這不會讓我的讀者對自身、對彼此、對這個季節，或對我感到厭煩。它也許會不時出沒在自己的宅邸鬧騰一番，然而不會有人祈禱它就此安息。

他們忠誠的朋友及僕人
查爾斯·狄更斯
一八四三年十二月

目錄

CONTENTS

第一樂章

馬利之魂

　　故事是這樣開始的：馬利死了；此乃毋庸置疑——牧師、教堂執事、葬儀社人員及主要的送葬者都已在埋葬登記簿上簽了名。史顧己也簽名了；在交易所裡，史顧己的簽名向來是種保證。所以，老馬利的確像釘死的門釘一樣僵死了。

　　別會錯意了！我這麼說並不代表我個人特別了解死氣沉沉的門釘。其實，我倒認為棺木釘才是最毫無生氣的金屬。但是這個比喻蘊含著我們老祖宗的智慧，並非我可以妄加褻瀆竄改的，否則這個國家豈不大亂？因此，就容我再強調一次吧：馬利已經像釘死的門釘一樣僵死了。

　　史顧己知道馬利死了嗎？那是當然的，他怎麼可能不知道呢？雖然我不曉得他們到底合夥了多久，但史顧己和馬利確實合夥了好多年。史顧己是馬利唯一的遺囑執行人、唯一的遺產管理人、唯一的遺產受讓人、唯一的遺產繼承人、唯一的朋友，也是唯一的送葬者。不過，史顧己並沒有為此嘔耗悲傷過度；葬禮當天，他依然維持自己精明商人的一貫本色，以不可思議的低價舉辦了隆重的喪禮。

　　提到馬利的葬禮，讓我又想起了故事開頭的那句話——

毋庸置疑，馬利死了。讀者必須確實了解這一點，否則我接下來要說的故事就不好玩了。要不是我們深信哈姆雷特的父王在拉開序幕前就去世，那麼，他在吹著東風的午夜時分到城牆上散步，又有什麼好奇怪的呢？因為，這只不過是個中年男人在夜晚輕率地跑到微風輕拂之處——如聖保羅墓地——去嚇嚇他兒子那脆弱的心靈罷了。

　　史顧己一直沒有塗掉老馬利的名字。好幾年過去了，老馬利的名字仍出現在店門上：史顧己與馬利。「史顧己與馬利」這行號已廣為人知。有時候，新顧客會稱史顧己為史顧己，有時則叫他馬利，而史顧己對這兩個稱謂都會回應——對他而言，兩者毫無差別。

　　噢！但他可是一個連石頭都能榨出油來的人哪，史顧己啊！是一個用擠、用撈、用刮、用貪、用摳，無論如何都要得到好處的老狐狸！他猶如又硬又尖的打火石，沒有任何鋼棒可以從他身上打出慷慨的火花；而且，他又宛若牡蠣一般神祕、封閉且孤僻。他內心的冷酷使他老朽的軀體蒙上一層寒霜，凍傷了他尖挺的鼻樑，冰皺了他的雙頰，冷僵了他的步伐，並使他雙眼通紅、薄唇發紫，連他那沙啞的聲音說出來的話語也十分冰冷刺骨。他的頭頂、眉骨及瘦削的下巴上，都覆蓋著白皚皚的寒霜。那股寒意總是與他如影隨形，即使是盛夏，他也可以讓辦公室的氣溫降至冰點，就算是聖誕節，情形依舊如此。

　　史顧己幾乎不受外界氣溫的影響。沒有任何的暖意可以溫暖他，也沒有任何冷慄的天氣可以叫他打寒顫。他比刺骨的寒風更為冷冽，比一心想降至人間的落雪更為冰冷，也比傾盆的暴雨更為無情。惡劣的天氣根本打不倒他。大雨、落雪或冰雹唯一贏得了他的是，至少它們經常大方地「布施」，史顧己可從來沒做過。

人們在街上碰到史顧己，從不會和顏悅色地對他寒暄：「親愛的史顧己，你好嗎？什麼時候要來我家坐坐？」沒有乞丐會向他乞求微薄的施捨，也沒有孩童會詢問他時間，更從未有人向他問路。盲人的導盲犬似乎也認得他，牠們看見他走來，會拖著主人轉進門廊或小巷裡，然後搖著尾巴，彷彿在說：「失明的主人啊！即使你失去雙眸，也強過擁有那雙邪惡的眼睛。」

但史顧己才不在乎呢！他樂得如此。對史顧己來說，循著擁擠的人生道路前進，並要那些富有同情心的人離遠一點兒，這可是聰明人口中所說的「樂事」呢。

有一天 —— 一年裡最美好的日子之一，也就是聖誕夜 —— 老史顧己正坐在他的帳房裡忙個不停。外面的天氣陰冷，寒風刺骨，濃霧瀰漫。史顧己可以聽到外頭巷弄裡的人們，喘著氣走來走去，還用掌擊胸、用力跺著人行道的鋪石來取暖。城裡的大鐘才剛敲過三點，但天色已相當昏暗了 —— 其實，這一整天的天色都不明亮 —— 隔壁辦公室的窗上燭光搖曳，恍若這片看似可以用手觸摸的灰褐空氣裡，多了些許紅色的汙漬。濃霧從縫隙及鑰匙孔湧入屋裡，而外頭更是一片霧茫茫，因此，儘管這條巷弄非常狹窄，對面的屋子看來卻像虛無的幻影。這一片骯髒的雲霧籠罩大地，並模糊萬物的景象，不禁讓人以為，造物者正在這附近釀造雲霧呢。

史顧己讓帳房的門大開，如此他才能監視他的職員，後者正在史顧己眼前那猶如水槽般陰暗狹小的房間裡抄寫信件。史顧己自己的爐火已經夠小了，但職員房裡的爐火更是小得不得了，好像只是擺在那的一塊煤炭罷了。但他卻沒有辦法添煤，因為史顧己將煤炭箱放在自己的帳房裡。所以，若職員拿著煤鏟進來想取煤炭，他的老闆就會暗示他可能得「走路」了。因此，職員只好披上自己的白羊毛圍巾，試圖就著蠟燭取暖；由於他的想像力不夠豐富，這種嘗試總是以失敗告終。

「舅舅，聖誕快樂！願上帝保佑你！」一陣欣喜雀躍的叫聲傳來，那是史顧己外甥的聲音。他以迅雷不及掩耳的速度闖入辦公室，史顧己聽見聲音才知道他來了。

「呸！」史顧己斥道：「亂來！」

因為剛從寒霧裡疾行而來，史顧己的外甥全身熱烘烘的，帥臉也紅撲撲的；他雙眼發亮，呼吸還冒著煙呢。「舅舅，你說聖誕節是亂來？」他叫道，「我想，你一定不是那個意思。」

「就是這個意思。」史顧己說，「聖誕快樂？你有什麼權利快樂？又有什麼理由快樂？你窮得可以了。」

「噢，拜託，」外甥仍愉悅地回話，「那你又有什麼權利不高興呢？又有何理由不開心？你夠富有了。」

史顧己一時找不出更好的回答，只好又說了一聲：「呸！」跟著又是一句：「亂來。」

「舅舅，別氣了！」外甥說。

「我能不氣嗎？這世界是如此愚蠢。」舅舅反問，「聖誕快樂！去他的聖誕快樂！聖誕節對你有什麼意義？對你來說，聖誕節不過是個提醒自己沒錢還債的時刻；不過是個發現自己又老了一歲、卻依然貧窮的時刻；不過是個要核對帳簿，卻發現每個月都是呆帳的日子罷了！假如我的願望能成真，」史顧己氣憤地說道，「每個把『聖誕快樂』掛在嘴邊的笨蛋，都應該跟他的布丁放到鍋裡一起蒸一下，並在他們胸口插根冬青木，然後埋了他們。就該這樣！」

「舅舅！」外甥求饒道。

「我的甥兒呀！」史顧己斷然地回答，「你去慶祝你的聖誕，也讓我過我自己的聖誕吧。」

「過聖誕！」史顧己的外甥重述了一次：「但你又沒有過聖誕！」

「那麼，就讓我不過節吧，」史顧己道，「但願聖誕節為你帶來許多好處！跟以前一樣，為你帶來許多好處！」

「我敢說，我能夠從很多事情當中獲得好處，儘管我沒有因此獲利，」外甥回應，「過聖誕節就是一個例子。每當聖誕節來臨，即使是撇開對它那神聖之名及起源的崇敬——

其實跟聖誕節有關的一切都脫離不了這份崇敬——我也總是把它當成一個好日子；一個友善的、寬恕的、慈悲的且歡樂的時刻；據我所知，在漫長的一年當中，唯有此刻，人們能暫時敞開緊閉的心胸，把比自己卑微的人當成人生旅途上的夥伴，而非不同世界的其他族群。因此，舅舅，儘管聖誕節沒替我的口袋添點金子或銀幣，但我相信它的確已給了我好處，以後也將帶給我好處。所以，我要說，上帝保佑！」

「水槽」裡的職員不由得鼓起掌來，但他隨即察覺此種行為不妥，於是他傾身假意撥了撥火，卻不小心把最後的微弱火星給弄熄了。

「你要是再讓我聽到任何聲音，」史顧己說，「你就好捲鋪蓋回去過聖誕節吧。」然後他轉向外甥諷刺地說道，「先生，我真好奇，你口才這麼好，怎麼不進國會當議員？」

「舅舅，別生氣啦。來吧！明天與我們一起共進晚餐吧。」

史顧己說他寧願看著他……不錯，他真的這麼說，說他寧可看他陷入絕境，也不去吃飯。

「為什麼？」史顧己的外甥喊道：「為什麼呢？」

「你為什麼會結婚？」史顧己問。

「因為我戀愛了。」

「因為你戀愛了！」史顧己咆哮起來，好像這是世界上唯一一比「聖誕快樂」更荒謬的一句話。

「再見！」

「舅舅，別這樣。我結婚前你也沒找過我，現在怎麼可以拿這當作明天不來的藉口呢？」

「再見。」史顧己說。

「我並不指望你給我任何好處，也不圖你什麼，為何我們不能好好相處呢？」

「再見。」史顧己說。

「看到您這麼堅決，我真的是打從心底感到難過。我們以前從未吵過架——我也不想這麼做——這次不過是為了表達我對聖誕節的崇敬罷。我會一直維持著我的聖誕好心情，所以，我還是要說，舅舅，聖誕快樂！」

「再見。」史顧己說。

「也祝您新年快樂！」

「再見。」史顧己說。

雖然如此，他的外甥仍毫無怨言地離開。他在外間的門邊稍作停留，好給予那位職員祝福，後者雖然渾身發冷，但仍比史顧己熱情，他衷心地回禮。

「另一個討厭鬼，」史顧己聽到職員回應外甥的話，咕噥道，「我這個員工一個禮拜才賺十五先令，還要養家糊口，他竟然也敢說聖誕快樂？我真的要進瘋人院了。」

這個瘋職員才剛送走史顧己的外甥，又迎了兩個人進來。他們是身材魁梧、相貌討喜的紳士，現在都脫下帽子，站在史顧己的帳房裡。他們手中拿著冊子與文件，向史顧己鞠躬。

　　其中一個人看了看名冊說：「我想，這裡就是『史顧己與馬利』了。我該尊稱您為史顧己先生，還是馬利先生呢？」

　　「馬利先生死七年了，」史顧己答道，「正是七年前的這個晚上去世的。」

　　「我們相信，他的合夥人一定會像他一樣慷慨施。」紳士一邊說道，一邊遞出他的證件。

　　的確，史顧己跟馬利一直很相像。一聽到「慷慨好施」這不祥的字眼，史顧己皺起眉頭，搖搖頭，將證件遞回去。

　　紳士拿起一枝筆，同時說道：「史顧己先生，在這一年之中最歡樂的時刻，我們更應該略盡綿薄之力來救濟那些正在受難的貧苦人家，此刻他們正需要援手。有許多人的日常所需相當匱乏，也有許多人連最起碼的溫飽都得不到呢，先生。」

　　「難道沒有監獄嗎？」史顧己問。

　　「很多呀。」紳士答道，筆也放了下來。

　　「那聯合貧民習藝所呢？」史顧己繼續詢問，「還存在嗎？」

　　「它們仍然存在，」紳士回答，「但我希望有天能說它們已經消失了。」

　　「還有『磨坊法案』與『濟貧法案』，都還在執行嗎？」

小氣財神

「兩者都在執行中，先生。」

「噢，聽到你剛才說的話，我還真擔心，以為發生了什麼事情讓這些政策停擺了。」史顧己說：「現在聽到你這麼說，我就安心了。」

「我們認為，這些政策根本不能讓世人在心靈或肉體上體驗身為基督徒的歡愉，」紳士說，「所以，我們一些人正努力募款，來為可憐的人們添購食物或禦寒的衣物。我們會選擇這個時間募款，是因為此刻窮人的需求迫在眉睫，而富者也樂意慷慨解囊。我該為你登記多少呢？」

「不用！」史顧己回答。

「你想匿名？」

「我希望能夠清靜點。」史顧己說：「先生，既然你問我有什麼願望，那以下就是我的回答：我自己不在聖誕節尋歡作樂，也不會花錢供那些懶惰蟲玩樂。我已經捐助很多錢到剛剛提到的那幾個機構了，窮人就該到那兒去。」

「但很多人進不去，還有更多人是寧死也不願進去。」

「假如他們寧願死的話，」史顧己道：「那就死了算了，這樣還可以緩解人口過剩的壓力。而且——抱歉——我對這些事不太懂。」

「但你該知道。」紳士發表意見。

「這不關我的事，」史顧己回答：「一個人只要清楚自己的事就夠了，用不著多管別人的閒事。更何況，我自己的事就忙不過來了。再見了，兩位。」

馬利之魂

這兩位紳士知道自己無法勸服史顧己，便離開了。史顧己重新埋頭工作，他對自己的表現相當滿意，心情也較平常輕鬆許多。

此時，霧氣漸濃，天色越來越暗，街上的人們拿著熊熊的火把跑在馬車前面，好幫忙引路。教堂的古老鐘樓——那已然聲嘶力竭的老鐘，總是愛透過牆上的哥德式玻璃偷窺史顧己——現在卻看不到了，只有在整點或一刻鐘時才能聽見雲層中傳來的鐘聲，其後帶著顫抖的餘音，好似是它的牙齒正在凍僵的腦袋瓜裡格格打顫。天氣越來越冷了。大街上屋宅的一隅，一些正在修理煤氣管的工人在火盆裡升起了熊熊火焰，而一群衣衫襤褸的大人小孩都圍攏過來暖手，高興地在火盆前眨眼。消防栓被孤零零地棄置一旁，溢流的水慍怒地凝結，凍成憤世嫉俗的冰塊。

商家燈火通明，櫥窗燈光的熱度烘得冬青枝木及漿果劈啪作響，也映紅了過往路人蒼白的面孔。家禽店與雜貨店人聲鼎沸，那熱鬧的場面真叫人難以相信，沒想到討價還價這無聊的手法此刻還能派上用場。擁有氣派豪宅的市長，下令他的五十個廚子及男管家準備出市長官邸該有的聖誕派頭。就連上個禮拜一才因為在街上酒醉鬧事，被罰了五先令的小裁縫師，也在自家的小閣樓裡攪拌著明天過節要吃的布丁，他瘦弱的妻子則與小孩外出買牛肉去了。

霧更濃，天也更冷了！椎心的酷寒！假如當初善良的聖鄧斯坦並非使出慣用的武器，而是用這刺骨的天氣來鉗住撒旦的鼻頭,那麼,撒旦想必會痛得呼天搶地吧。嚴寒像狗啃骨頭般地嚙咬著一個孩童小巧的鼻子,這個孩子正湊著史顧己的鑰匙孔唱出聖誕歡頌:「愉悅的紳士啊,上帝保佑你!祝你無憂無慮!」

但他才唱出第一句,史顧己就恨恨地抓起長尺,嚇得那位唱歌的孩童落荒而逃,把鑰匙孔讓給了濃霧,更確切地說是,寒霜。

終於,下班時間到了。史顧己不情願地自板凳上起身,沉默地示意水槽間的職員可以離開了。期待已久的職員立刻吹熄蠟燭,戴上帽子。

「我猜,你希望明天可以放假吧?」史顧己說道。

「是的,老闆,如果方便的話。」

「不方便,」史顧己說道,「而且也不公平。我想,如果我因此扣你半克朗的薪水,你會覺得自己吃虧了吧?」

職員有氣無力地笑了笑。

「但是,」史顧己說:「你沒來上班,我還得照付你薪水,你倒不認為我吃虧。」

職員辯駁說一年也只有這麼一次。

「利用十二月二十五號來扒人家口袋的錢?這個藉口太爛了!」史顧己把大衣的釦子直扣到下巴,同時說道:「不過,我想,還是讓你休假一天吧!後天早上可得早點到。」

職員答應後,史顧己便嘀咕著走出門外。辦公室的門瞬間就被關上了,職員披上了白色羊毛圍巾,長長的圍巾垂至腰際（因為他沒有大衣），然後尾隨一群男孩，沿著康伊爾街的斜坡高興地滑行，為了慶祝聖誕夜，他來來回回滑了二十幾次，最後，他才儘快衝回在康登鎮的家，準備跟家人玩捉迷藏。

史顧己則到他經常光顧的那家昏暗的小酒店裡享用他陰鬱的晚餐；他讀完所有的報紙後，又拿出帳簿來消磨剩下的時光，最後才回家睡覺。他居住的公寓原屬於他死去的合夥人所有，裡頭盡是一間間暗無天日的房間。這棟高大的建築物聳立在院子裡，感覺如此地孤單荒涼，叫人禁不住猜想，它是不是在年輕時，跟其他房子玩捉迷藏躲到這裡，結果卻忘了出去的路。這棟建築現在已十分老舊冷清，因為只有史顧己住在裡面，其餘的房間全都出租當辦公室使用了。此時院子裡一片漆黑，即使是對它瞭若指掌的史顧己，也不得不在黑暗中伸手摸索。濃霧與寒氣瀰漫著暗黑古舊的屋門口，恍若天氣之神正坐在門檻上哀傷地沉思著。

事實上，門上的門環除了奇大無比外，並無任何特殊之處。史顧己每天都見得著這個門環；而且，就如同多數的倫敦人——大膽點來說，這包括了市政府、地方官及同業工會的會員——史顧己的想像力十分貧乏。

值得注意的還有一點：史顧己除了那天下午曾提過去世七年的老合夥人，接下來壓根兒就沒再想到馬利。那麼，誰能跟我解釋，為什麼在史顧己將鑰匙插入鑰匙孔時，看到的門環——門環本身並未有過任何修改——忽然變成了馬利的

臉呢？

　　馬利的臉。它不像院子裡的其他東西一般陰陰暗暗，在它四周有一道微弱的光圈，就像是一隻放在黑暗地窖裡的腐爛龍蝦。這張臉並沒有任何憤怒或猙獰的神情，只是以馬利常有的眼神看著史顧己。它的額頭上戴著一副詭異的眼鏡，頭髮散亂得有一點怪，看來像是一股氣息或熱氣的傑作。儘管它的眼睛大睜，卻是眨也不眨，再加上那死白的臉色，使整張臉看起來很是駭人；不過，儘管這張臉看來可怕，但那可怕的氣息卻非臉本身所能造就的，而是臉部表情以外的氣氛所致。

　　史顧己正要定睛細看時，它卻又變成門環了。

　　若要說史顧己沒有被嚇到，或說他並未感受到前所未有的恐懼，那是騙人的。但他仍然用剛縮回的那隻手插入鑰匙，堅定地開了鎖，走進屋子裡，然後點上蠟燭。

　　然而，關上門之前，他的確猶疑了一下，也的確先小心翼翼地檢視了門的背面，似乎害怕看到馬利的辮子出現在門背上。但門後除了釘著門環的螺絲釘外，並沒有任何東西，所以他「呸」了兩聲後，便用力地甩上門。

　　關門聲雷鳴似地在屋子裡頭隆隆迴響。樓上的每個房間，還有樓下地窖裡酒商的酒桶，似乎都傳出回聲。史顧己才不怕回聲呢，他鎖緊門，走過大廳，然後一邊修剪蠟燭的燭芯，一邊慢慢地走上樓梯。

　　你大可含糊其詞地說，有人能夠駕著一輛六駕馬車爬上老舊的樓梯，或穿過剛出爐卻充滿紕漏的國會法案漏洞；但我想說的是，你的確可以駕著一台靈柩車爬上這段樓梯，甚至可以橫著開上來，讓車前的橫木向著牆，車門朝著欄杆，輕鬆地上樓。樓梯的寬度不但足夠，而且還有多餘的空間；或許這也是為什麼史顧己會認為，他在黑暗中看到一輛靈柩車走在他前頭。外頭街上的那六盞煤氣燈連門口都照不明了，所以，你可以想見，光是靠史顧己那一丁點的燭火，四周會有多暗了。

史顧己絲毫不以為意，繼續往上爬。黑暗意味著不用花錢，這正是史顧己所喜歡的。但在關上重重的房門前，他還是巡視了各個房間，以確保一切安好。因為想到剛才那張臉，他就覺得必須這麼做。

客廳、臥房、儲藏室，老樣子。桌子或沙發底下沒有人，壁爐裡有著小小的火焰；湯匙及碗盆都放好了；用來煮粥的小鍋子（因為史顧己有點傷風）好端端地放在鍋架上。沒人躲在床下、衣櫥裡，牆上懸掛的睡袍雖然樣子怪怪的，但也沒有人躲在裡邊。儲藏室也一如往常，裡面放著老舊的爐柵、舊鞋、兩只魚簍、一個三腳盥洗台和一把火鉗。

史顧己滿意地關上門，將自己鎖在房內；不過，他上了兩道鎖，這不是他一貫的作風。感到安心後，他取下領結，換上睡袍及拖鞋，戴上睡帽，隨後就坐在爐火前吃起粥來。

爐火真的非常微弱，在這酷寒的夜晚根本起不了任何作用。史顧己只好挨近一點，盡量傾身朝向爐火，才能從這一

小塊的煤炭中獲取些許暖意。這個老舊的壁爐是某個荷蘭商人好久以前打造的，它的四周鋪滿了稀奇美麗的荷蘭磁磚，描繪了一些聖經故事的圖案：有該隱和亞伯、法老的女兒、示巴皇后、降臨至羽絨被般的雲層上的天使、亞伯拉罕、伯沙撒、搭著奶油船出海的基督使徒，以及數百個能吸引史顧己的人物。然而，馬利那張死了七年的臉孔，卻像古老先知的手杖般，吞噬了一切。假如每塊磁磚上頭本是一片空白，而史顧己零亂的思緒又能夠浮映其上的話，那每塊磁磚上頭出現的一定都是老馬利的頭像。

「神經病！」史顧己說著，並在房裡踱起步來。

轉了幾圈後，他又坐下。他將頭靠在椅背上時，正巧瞥見掛在房內的廢棄搖鈴，這個搖鈴與頂樓的房間相通，當初設置的原因早已為人淡忘了。而現在，令史顧己驚訝不已且感到莫名恐懼的是，搖鈴晃了起來。起初晃得很慢，沒有發出任何聲音；沒多久，鈴聲大作，同時，房子裡面所有的搖鈴都跟著響了起來。

這情形大約持續了三十秒或一分鐘，但感覺卻像是過了一小時之久。剛剛一同響起的鈴聲，現在又同時停止了，取而代之的是樓下傳來叮叮噹噹的噪音，就像樓下酒商的酒窖裡，有人正拖著鐵鍊走在酒桶上一樣。然後，史顧己想起，曾經聽過人家形容鬼屋裡的鬼都是拖著鐵鍊的。

酒窖的門「砰」的一聲打開了，樓下的噪音越來越大，接著便傳到樓梯，直朝他的房門而來。

「見鬼了！」史顧己道：「我才不相信這些呢。」

然而，當鬼魂暢行無礙地穿過厚重的房門，出現在他的面前時，史顧己終究還是臉色大變。它一進來，原本快要熄滅的火焰突然劈里啪啦地燃燒起來，彷彿正在叫嚷著：「我知道它！那是馬利的鬼魂！」之後，火焰又再度暗了下去。

同樣的臉，一模一樣。馬利綁著髮辮，穿著往日常穿的背心、緊身褲和皮靴，鞋子上頭的流蘇跟他的髮辮、衣緣及頭上的頭髮一樣，都豎立起來。他的腰部緊扣著一串很長的鐵鍊，像條尾巴似地纏繞著他；（根據史顧己的詳細觀察）這串鐵鍊是由保險箱、鑰匙、鎖蕊、帳簿、契約及精密厚重的鋼鐵錢袋串成的。馬利渾身透明，所以史顧己可以看穿他的背心，瞧見衣服後面的兩顆鈕子。

過去，史顧己時常聽人家說馬利沒有心肝，但直到此刻他才信了這句話。不，即使是現在，他也無法置信。雖然，他徹底地看到了幻影，看到它站在他面前；雖然，他正因為那雙死氣沉沉的眼睛而猛打冷顫；雖然，他也注意到繫在鬼魂頭上及下巴上的圍巾，是他從未見過的質地；但是，他仍舊無法置信，依然想否決自己的感覺。

「怎麼了？」史顧己口氣一如往常地苛刻及冷漠，「你有什麼事嗎？」

「多著呢！」無須懷疑，那的確是馬利的聲音。

「你是誰？」

「你該問我過去是誰。」

「那麼，你過去是誰？」史顧己拉高聲調，「你用字真講究──就鬼而言。」他本想說「當鬼還那麼挑剔」，但最終還是選擇了較恰當的說法。

　　「我生前是你的合夥人，雅各‧馬利。」

　　「你能坐下來嗎？」史顧己問道，並以懷疑的眼光目視著它。

　　「可以。」

　　「那麼，坐吧。」

　　史顧己會這麼問，是因為他不知道這透明的鬼魂是否能夠就坐；他想，假如鬼魂無法坐下的話，它還得尷尬地解釋一番。但這鬼魂輕而易舉地面對壁爐坐下，好似這是習以為常的動作。

　　「你不相信我的存在。」鬼魂觀察道。

　　「我是不相信。」史顧己說。

　　「除了你的感覺，你還要什麼證據來證明我的存在？」

　　「我也不知道。」史顧己說。

　　「為何你要懷疑自己的感覺呢？」

　　「因為，」史顧己回答，「感覺會因一些小事而改變。肚子裡一點小小的不舒服就會影響感覺。你很可能只是一小塊未消化的牛肉、一口芥茉、一小片起士或是一塊半生不熟的馬鈴薯。不管你是什麼東西，說你是鬼，還不如說你可能是凝結成形的肉汁。」

　　史顧己不習慣說笑，現在心裡也沒有開玩笑的念頭。事實上，他只是試圖裝得很機靈，好分散注意力來壓制自身的恐懼，因為鬼魂的聲音已讓他感到毛骨悚然了。

片刻的沉默中，光是呆坐著對視那雙不會轉動的眼睛，就讓史顧己覺得渾身不對勁。此外，鬼魂身上陰森森的氣息也很恐怖。史顧己自己是沒有感覺，但事實上確實如此：即使鬼魂穩穩地坐著不動，它的頭髮、衣緣及流蘇都像有蒸氣吹拂般不停飄動。

「你看見這根牙籤了吧？」史顧己很快又重新出招；就像剛提到的，他希望那呆滯的目光能離開自己身上，即使只有片刻。

「看到了。」鬼魂答道。

「你並沒有看著它。」史顧己說。

「但我看得到它。」鬼魂道。

「噢，」史顧己回嘴：「我若吞下這根牙籤，下半輩子鐵定會被一堆我自己想像出來的妖魔小鬼所折磨。胡來，我跟你說──胡來！」

聽到這，鬼魂忽然發出了恐怖的尖叫，同時搖動身上的鐵鍊，發出令人聞之喪膽的陰慘聲音。史顧己嚇得捉緊椅背，以防自己昏厥。但是，更讓他恐懼的是，鬼魂似乎覺得屋內太熱，於是它摘下頭巾，下巴卻因此掉到了胸前。

史顧己嚇得腿軟並跪倒在地，用手搗著臉。

「神啊！」史顧己叫道，「恐怖的幽靈哪，你為什麼要來煩我？」

「你這世俗之輩！」鬼魂答道，「你現在相信我的存在了嗎？」

「我相信，」史顧己回答，「我不得不相信。但為什麼你會出現？又為什麼找上我？」

「每個人體內的靈魂都需要在人間遊蕩四方；」鬼魂答道，「假如它在生前沒有這樣做，那死後也得這麼做。四處遊蕩漂泊——噢，我多麼可憐啊！——見證那些它過去本該與人分享並得到的歡樂，但現在卻已無法分享的事物。」

鬼魂又嚎叫了一聲，它搖動鐵鍊並緊握自己虛幻的雙手。

「告訴我，你身上的鐵鍊又是怎麼回事？」史顧己顫抖地問。

「這鐵鍊是我在世時鑄造的，」鬼魂答道，「是我自己一環一環、一段又一段地打造出來的；我自願纏繞著它，將來也自願戴著它。難道它的樣式對你來說陌生嗎？」

史顧己抖得越來越厲害。

「還是你想知道，」鬼魂咄咄逼人地說道，「你的鐵鍊有多重多長？在七年前的聖誕夜，你的鐵鍊就跟我的一樣重一樣長了。在那之後，你又為它加工不少；現在，你的鐐銬已沉重無比。」

史顧己瞄了瞄地板，以為會看到自己周圍有五六十呎長的鐵鍊，但什麼也沒看到。

「雅各，」史顧己哀求道，「老雅各·馬利，再多說一點。說些安慰的話吧，雅各！」

「埃比尼澤·史顧己，我沒辦法安慰你，」鬼魂回答，「安慰的話來自另一個領域，由另一種使者傳遞給另一種人。我也無法告訴你我要做什麼，我所獲准能做的事很少很少。我不能在任何地方休息、耽擱或逗留。我的靈魂從未離開我們的帳房——注意聽我說——生前，我的鬼魂從未離開過我們那窄小的錢坑，如今前頭還有非常漫長的旅程在等著我。」

史顧己將手插進褲子後頭的口袋裡——每當他心有所思時，就會出現這個習慣動作。

現在，史顧己便將手插進褲袋裡，邊想著鬼魂所說的話，但他並沒有抬起眼或站起身。

「雅各，你一定是動作太慢了。」史顧己一本正經地說道，語氣卻又帶著謙虛與尊重。

「太慢了？」鬼魂重複史顧己的話。

「死了七年，」史顧己若有所思地說，「卻一直在遊蕩？」

「整整七年，」鬼魂說，「沒有休息。不得安寧，不停地受到悔恨的折磨。」

「你移動的速度很快嗎？」史顧己道。

「如乘風而行。」鬼魂回答。

「那這七年內，你一定去了許多地方。」史顧己說。鬼魂一聽，又發出一聲哀號，又把鐵鍊晃得哐啷哐啷作響，在死寂的黑夜中聽來特別恐怖，守夜的人若聽到了，絕對會告他妨礙安寧。

「噢！受到束縛、給上了層層鐐銬的人呀，」鬼魂叫道，「並不知道千百年來人們一直在為這地球付出心力，只為了想完整地發揮這地球上的美德，讓努力成為永恆；也不知道每個基督徒的靈魂都在自己小小的世界裡——無論範圍多小——努力地行善，他們只恨人生苦短，無法盡情行善；更不知道，再多的悔恨也彌補不了一個人白白錯失的機會。我過去就是這樣！噢，我就是這樣！」

「可是，雅各，你事業很成功啊。」史顧己諂媚道，他現在開始將狀況套到自己身上來。

「事業！」鬼魂叫了起來，再度緊握雙手，「人類才是我的事業。眾人的福祉就是我的事業，慈善、憐憫、寬容及善心就是我的事業。在我廣闊的事業中，那些商業交易只不過是滄海一粟罷了。」

鬼魂舉起手上的鐵鍊，然後，就像那些鐵鍊是悔恨的來源似，他又重重地將鐵鍊摔到地面。

「時光周而復始，」鬼魂說，「每年這個時節我最痛苦。為什麼以前我走在人群裡總是低垂著雙眼，不曾抬起頭，瞧瞧那引領三位智者前往聖人誕生之簡陋處所的星星呢？難道我周遭沒有任何貧困的人家，是值得星星指引我前往的！」

鬼魂這樣不停地說，讓史顧己不禁感到膽寒，他開始發抖。

「聽我說！」鬼魂叫道，「我快沒時間了。」

「我在聽，」史顧己說，「但不要對我太凶！求求你！雅各，不要再說那些話了！」

「我不會告訴你，為何要讓你見到我。我在你身旁隱形好久了。」

這聽來讓人不甚愉快。史顧己顫慄著，拭掉眉頭上的汗滴。

「我的懲罰一點都不好受，」鬼魂繼續說道，「我來這裡是為了警告你，你還有一絲機會及希望避開與我相同的宿命。埃比尼澤，這是我特地為你爭取的機會與希望。」

「你一直是我的好朋友，」史顧己說，「感謝你。」

「你會遇到三個精靈。」鬼魂繼續往下說。

史顧己的臉色一沉，幾乎與鬼魂剛剛掉下來的下巴一樣低。

「雅各，這就是你所說的機會與希望嗎？」他支支吾吾地問。

「不錯。」

「那我想，我寧願不要。」史顧己說。

「如果沒有它們，」鬼魂說，「你就無可避免地要重蹈我的覆轍了。明天凌晨一點的鐘聲響起時，第一個精靈就會出現了。」

「雅各，我不能同時與三個精靈會面，然後一次解決嗎？」史顧己暗示道。

「第二個精靈會在第二天的同一時間出現，最後一位則
會在第三天十二點的鐘聲停止時出現。你不會再見到我了；
而且，為了你自己好，你最好記得我們之間所發生的事
情。」

鬼魂說完這些話，便抓起桌上的頭巾，跟之前一樣將它
纏繞至自己頭上。聽到鬼魂牙齒所發出來的聲音，史顧己便
知道它的下巴又因頭巾而聚合在一起了。他再度冒險地抬起
眼，發現面前這位超自然的訪客已站起身，手上的鐵鍊仍一
圈圈地纏繞其上。

鬼魂倒退著離開；它每後退一步，後面的窗子就會打開
一些，當它退到窗邊時，窗戶已全然打開了。

鬼魂示意史顧己靠近，史顧己照辦了。當他們相距兩步
時，馬利的鬼魂舉起手警告他不要再靠近，史顧己因而停下
腳步。

這倒不是出於順從，而是因為驚訝與害怕。因為鬼魂一
舉起手，史顧己就聽到空氣中有著惱人的噪音：那是相當不
和諧的痛哭與懊悔聲，那是難以形容的哀戚與自我譴責。鬼
魂聽了一會兒後，也加入這哀傷的輓歌，向外飄進了荒涼的
黑夜。

史顧己在好奇心的驅使下，走到窗邊朝外望。

空氣中充滿著鬼魅，它們一刻也不停地四處奔走，一邊
還發出嗚咽的呻吟。每個鬼魂都跟馬利一樣，身戴鐵鍊，有

些（它們可能是可惡的政府）則被銬在一起；每個鬼魂都不得自由。有許多人生前都是史顧己認識的：他跟一個穿著白色背心、腳踝上銬著大型鐵製保險箱的老鬼魂很熟，這個鬼魂看到下方的門階上有一位抱著嬰兒的貧窮婦女時，因自己無法給予幫助而哀號。這些鬼魂的痛苦顯然都是因為它們想要助人，但死後的它們已永遠失去這項能力了。

史顧己無法弄清，到底是這些鬼魂沒入了濃霧中，還是霧氣掩蓋了它們。總之，這些鬼魂及哭聲都一塊兒消失了，夜晚又恢復成他剛才回家時的模樣。

史顧己關上窗戶，察看鬼魂進來的那扇門。門上兩道他親手鎖上的鎖絲毫沒有被動過，門閂也沒有異狀。史顧己很想要說一聲「胡來」，但才說出第一個字就住嘴了。或許是經歷了剛剛的刺激，或許是一整天下來的疲憊，或許是他無意地窺見了未知的世界，或許是與馬利鬼魂的枯冗對話，也或許是夜深了；總之，史顧己急需休息。他直走到床前，還來不及寬衣解帶，就立刻倒下睡著了。

第二樂章
第一個精靈

史顧已醒來時，夜仍漆黑，他幾乎分不清透明的玻璃窗和屋內昏暗的牆壁。他機警的雙眼竭力地在黑暗中探查，而此時，鄰近的教堂響起整點的鐘聲，於是他細耳傾聽時間。

令他大為詫異的是，沉重的鐘聲竟然響了六下至七下，再從七下打到八下，就這樣規律地響了十二下才停止。十二下！他上床時都過了兩點了。那個鐘鐵定壞了，一定是冰柱害的！十二下！

他按下打簧錶的彈簧，想看看教堂的鐘錯得多離譜。彈簧輕巧快速地跳動了十二下才停下來。

「天啊，不可能，」史顧已喃喃道，「我不可能睡了一整個白天，又睡到半夜。可是也不可能說太陽出了毛病，現在其實是中午十二點吧。」

這想法令人感到不對勁，他爬下床，摸索著走到窗邊。他不得不先用睡袍的袖子擦掉窗戶上的霧氣，如此才能看見窗外的風景，不過能見度依舊相當低。他所能辨識的只有：外面仍是一片霧濛濛，天氣依舊寒冷，街上聽不見人來人往的喧鬧聲，恍若黑夜已擊敗白晝，接管了這個世界。這想法倒讓人感到快慰，因為若沒有日子可以數數的話，那「見票即支付埃比尼澤・史顧己先生」等等的話就變成了美國州政府的擔保，可以耍賴。

史顧己再次爬上床，他絞盡腦汁，但仍想不出個所以然來。他越想越困惑；越試著避免去想，就想得越多。馬利的鬼魂縈繞在他的腦中。每當他深思熟慮，斷定一切只不過是一場夢時，心思卻又像放開的彈簧，再度彈回原點，然後同樣的問題又擺在眼前：「這究竟是不是一場夢呢？」

史顧己就這樣一直躺著，直到鐘敲了三刻鐘，他才突然想到，馬利的鬼魂曾經警告他，一點的鐘聲響起時，會有精靈來拜訪他。他決心清醒地躺著，等待時間過去。況且，現在要他入睡簡直比登天還難，所以這或許是最明智之舉了。

這一刻鐘非常地漫長，讓他一度以為，他可能不自覺地打了個盹，錯過了時間。最後，鐘聲終於響了。

「叮咚！」

「一刻鐘。」史顧己數著。

「叮咚！」

「半點鐘。」史顧己說。

「叮咚！」

「三刻鐘。」史顧己說。

「叮咚！」

「整點，」史顧己得意地說，「根本沒事嘛！」

他說話時，整點的鐘聲其實還沒響，之後，沉悶、單調、空洞且陰鬱的整點鐘聲才響起。剎那間，房間亮了起來，他的床帷也給拉了開來。

　　我可以告訴讀者，他的床帷是給一隻手拉開的。被拉開的不是他腳邊的床帷，也不是他身後的，而是他面前的床帷。他的床帷給拉到一旁，而史顧已半撐起身子，發現自己正面對著拉下床帷的神秘訪客；就如同我跟你之間的距離一樣近，而我的靈魂現正在你的手肘邊呢。

　　這個訪客的形體很奇特——像個孩子：但它的模樣卻更像個老頭，只因為藉由某種超自然媒介出現，而讓自己的外形縮小許多，身體的比例像個孩子似的。他恍若因上了年紀而花白的頭髮披在頸後，直落到背部；不過，它的臉上沒有一絲皺紋，肌膚柔嫩極了；手臂長而結實，手掌也一樣，就像拳頭般力量奇大無比；纖細的雙腿與雙腳，則跟上肢一樣赤裸。它穿著潔白的長袍，腰際繫著一條色澤美麗的皮帶。另外，它手中持有一枝青翠的冬青木；而與象徵寒冬的冬青木呈現出強烈對比的是，它的衣服飾有盛夏的花朵。但最奇怪的是，它頭頂散發出一道明亮清晰的光芒，照亮了一切，腋下則夾有一頂帽子，無疑地，這頂帽子具有滅光的功能，在它戴上後可以掩蓋住頭頂的光芒。

　　然而，當史顧已益發凝神地注視著它時，卻發現這還不是它最特別的地方。因為，當它的皮帶一會兒這邊閃、一下子那邊亮地明滅不定時，精靈的身體也隨之有著變化：有時只有一隻手，一下子只剩一隻腿，一會兒又生出二十條腿，有時又變成只有一雙腿卻沒有頭的模樣，隨後又馬上成了只有頭沒有身體的樣子；那些消失的部分在這濃密的黑暗中融化了，根本看不到輪廓。奇妙的是，它再次恢復原樣，而且一如之前地清晰。

「先生，你就是那預定要來找我的精靈吧？」史顧己詢問道。

「是的。」

它的聲音輕柔且溫和，非常地低沉，就像是從遠方傳來的聲音。

「你是誰？你要做什麼呢？」

「我是過去的聖誕精靈。」

「很久以前？」史顧己見它身材矮小，忍不住又問。

「不，是你的過去而已。」

或許，史顧己自己也說不出理由，但他突然想看看精靈戴上帽子的模樣，於是他央求它這麼做。

「什麼！」精靈尖叫起來：「你這麼快就想要以世俗的雙手來掩蓋我所給予的光芒？都是你跟其他的同類打造出這頂帽子，並且強迫我帽子低低地戴了好幾年，這還不夠嗎？」

史顧己誠心地表示毫無冒犯之意，也表明自己有生之年未曾強迫精靈「戴帽子」。接著，他又大膽地詢問精靈來此的目的。

「為了你的幸福！」精靈說。

史顧己表示自己不勝感激，但忍不住想，若能好好睡一晚不受打擾，他會覺得更幸福。精靈顯然聽見了他的想法，因為它立刻說：「那麼，就算是為了你的改過自新吧。注意了！」

精靈一面說著，一面伸出強壯的手，輕輕地抓起史顧己的手臂。

「起來，跟我一起走！」

儘管史顧己哀求說，現在的天氣與時間不宜散步；說床鋪很溫暖，而且溫度計指著零下好幾度；說自己穿得很單薄，只有拖鞋、睡衣及睡帽；說自己正感冒病著——一切仍是徒勞。捉著他的手雖然輕柔如女子，卻令人無法反抗。他只好起身，但一發現精靈正朝窗戶走去，他便緊抓住自己的長袍哀求。

「我只是個凡人，」史顧己抗議道，「我會摔死的。」精靈將手放到史顧己胸口：「只要碰碰我這裡的手，你就能夠飛翔了。」

話一說完，他們就穿牆而過，站在一條寬闊的鄉間大道上，兩旁盡是田野。整個城市都消失了，完全看不到蛛絲馬跡。黑夜與濃霧也已消散，取而代之的是清爽寒冷的冬日，皚皚白雪覆蓋著地面。

「我的天啊！」史顧己張望四周，緊握著雙手說：「這是我出生的地方，是我度過童年的地方。」

精靈和善地注視著他。即使只有一下子，但它溫柔的眼神似乎觸動了史顧己。他感覺到空氣中飄浮著數千種氣味，

第二個精靈

每一種味道都足以勾起數千個他早已忘懷的念頭、希望、歡樂及牽掛。

「你的嘴唇在顫抖哪，」精靈說道，「你臉頰上出現的東西又是什麼？」

史顧己以異常的聲音咕噥說那只是一個膿皰，又求精靈帶他到他要去的地方。

「你記得路？」精靈問。

「當然記得！」史顧己熱烈地叫了起來，「矇著眼都認得。」

「真奇怪，那你卻遺忘了這麼多年，」精靈說，「我們走吧。」

他們沿著大道走。史顧己認得每扇門、每根柱子和每棵樹。最後，遠方出現了一座小城鎮，鎮上有橋、教堂及蜿蜒的河流。一些男孩騎著毛茸茸的小馬朝他們奔來，並一邊朝著坐在農人駕駛的雙輪馬車與貨車裡的男孩呼叫。這些男孩各個精神抖擻，高聲叫嚷著，使這廣闊的田野充滿了歡樂的聲音，連乾爽的空氣也不禁笑了。

「這些只是過去的幻影，」精靈說道，「他們感覺不到我們的存在。」

歡樂的旅人來了；當他們靠近時，史顧己認得並可以叫出每個人的名字。為什麼見著他們，他會欣喜若狂？為什麼他們經過時，他冷漠的雙眼會因而閃耀發光，心會怦怦地跳呢？為什麼那些旅人在十字路口分道揚鑣並互道聖誕快樂時，他會感到無比歡喜？聖誕快樂對史顧己來說算什麼？去他的聖誕快樂！它給過他什麼好處呢？

「學校裡還有人，」精靈說道，「有個被朋友忽略的孤單孩子，正一個人留在那裡。」

史顧己說他知道，然後啜泣起來。

他們離開大馬路，走上史顧己記憶深刻的小徑，很快地來到一座紅磚屋前，屋頂的圓頂塔上置有一支風信雞，屋簷則垂掛著一口銅鐘。這幢房子很大，但顯然已經老舊不堪了：好幾間寬闊的廚房及貯藏室都少有人使用，裡面的牆壁潮濕生苔，窗子都破了，門也壞了。有幾隻雞咕咕叫著，在馬廄裡昂首闊步；馬房及棚架上長滿了雜草。屋裡也同樣前景不再：一走進淒涼的大廳，環視各個敞開的房門後，他們發現這些房間設備簡陋，既冷清又空蕩；空氣中有著泥土的味道，那蕭條荒涼的感覺，讓人不禁想起從前秉著燭光起床，卻找不到足夠食物充飢的情形。

精靈與史顧己穿過大廳，來到屋後的一扇門前。門敞開著，露出一個狹長、簡陋又陰森的房間，幾張老舊的板凳及書桌使其更顯淒清。一個男孩坐在書桌前，正靠著微弱的爐火讀書。史顧己在板凳上坐下來，流淚望著他早已忘懷的年少身影。

屋裡潛伏的回聲，牆壁嵌板中老鼠的吱叫聲與混戰聲，後方蕭條院子裡的半凍水管所發出的滴答聲，為了葉子枯落而消沉的白楊樹所發出的嘆息聲，空房間的門所發出的單調

第一個精靈

轉動聲，火焰所發出的爆裂聲，聲聲都打進了史顧己的心中，讓他心一柔，淚水不斷從眼眶滑落。

精靈碰碰他的手臂，指著那正專心唸書的少年。突然之間，一個身穿異國服裝的男人——看來非常真切清楚——隔著窗站在外頭，他的腰間繫著一把戰斧，還牽著一匹載滿木柴的驢子。

「天啊，是阿里巴巴！」史顧己高興地大叫：「那是親愛又正直的老阿里巴巴！對，對，我知道！有一次聖誕節，那個孤單的小孩又獨自留在這裡時，阿里巴巴來過——那是他第一次來——就是那個樣子。可憐的孩子！」史顧己又說：「還有聖汎倫泰跟他野蠻的弟弟歐爾森，他們從那邊走過去啦！呃，那個人叫什麼名字？那個只穿著一條內褲，在睡夢中被抬到大馬士革城門口的人？你沒看到他嗎？還有，蘇丹的馬夫被妖怪倒吊起來了，你看那邊，他被倒吊著呢！活該！我真高興看到他這副模樣，他根本就沒資格娶公主。」

他倫敦商界的朋友若聽到史顧己如此又笑又叫地熱烈談論這類話題，或看到他發亮興奮的臉龐，不大吃一驚才怪呢。

「那隻鸚鵡在那裡！」史顧己喊起來，「綠身體與黃尾巴，頭頂有一撮萵苣般的東西，就是那隻沒錯！可憐的魯濱遜，他漂流多年回到家時，那隻鸚鵡對他說：『可憐的魯濱遜，你去了哪裡呢？魯濱遜。』魯濱遜還以為自己在作夢呢，但其實並不是。你知道的，就是那隻鸚鵡。還有那個星期五啊，拚命地跑向小海灣。嘿，加油，加油啊！」

隨後，他一反平日的習性，開始自憐起來：「可憐的孩子！」他又哭了。

「我希望……」史顧己用袖口揩拭眼淚後，將手插入口袋，環顧一下四周，繼而喃喃說道：「但現在已經太遲了。」

「什麼？」精靈問。

「沒什麼，」史顧己回答：「沒事。只是昨晚有個孩子在我門前唱耶誕歌，我應該給他一點回饋的，就這樣。」

精靈體貼地微笑，揮揮手說：「讓我們看看另一個聖誕節吧。」

它這麼一說，史顧己年少的身影便大了些，而房間也更暗更髒了。牆壁嵌板縮小了，窗戶也有了裂縫，天花板的石灰碎片掉了下來，裡頭的鋼條露了出來。這個景象是怎麼變的，史顧己也不比我們清楚。他只知道，眼前這個景象很真切，跟過去一樣；而且年少的史顧己又獨自留在那裡，其他的孩子都開心地回家過節了。

年少的史顧己這次並沒有在唸書，他頹喪地來回踱步。史顧己看看精靈，然後哀傷地搖搖頭，焦急地望向門口。

門開了，一個較男孩年幼的女孩衝了進來，她雙手環抱住他的頸子，不停地親吻他，並叫著：「親愛的，親愛的哥哥。」

第二個精靈

　　「親愛的哥哥，我是來接你回家去的！」女孩一邊說，一邊拍著瘦弱的小手，並且笑彎了腰：「我來接你回家呢，回家，回家！」

　　「回家？小芬妮？」男孩回問她。

　　「對啊！」女孩滿溢歡樂之情，說道：「回家，再也不離開了！永遠都待在家裡。爸爸比以前溫柔多了，所以家裡像座天堂。有一個甜蜜的夜晚，我要上床睡覺時，他很溫柔地對我說話，所以我就大膽問他可不可以讓你回家。他回答可以，你應該回家，並且讓我搭馬車來接你。你已經是個大人了！」女孩張大了眼睛說道：「你再也不用回這裡來了。不過，我們會先一起歡度聖誕節，享受世界上最美好的時光。」

　　「小芬妮，妳長大了。」男孩喊道。

　　她拍拍手笑著，試著要摸摸男孩的頭，但卻搆不到，於是她又笑起來，並墊著腳尖擁抱他。然後，她帶著稚氣的急切，拉著他朝門外走；他也很心甘情願地跟著她走。

　　大廳裡響起一陣駭人的叫聲：「把史顧己同學的箱子拿下來，放在那裡！」大廳裡，校長出現了，他帶著令人害怕的親切看著史顧己，還跟他握手，讓史顧己感到畏懼。接著，校長將史顧己與他的妹妹帶到一間老舊冰冷的接客室，裡頭牆上的地圖與窗邊的天象儀及地球儀都覆蓋著冰霜。校長拿出一瓶淡得出奇的酒及一塊硬蛋糕，分給面前的兩位年輕人，同時還派了一位瘦弱的僕人前去問車夫要不要喝點東

西，車夫表示他很感激，但若要喝的是跟之前相同的東西，
那他寧可不要。史顧己的行李已經安放在四輪馬車上，他們
高高興興地向校長道別，然後上了馬車。馬車興高采烈地駛
過花園彎道，車輪快速地奔馳，濺起了常青樹深色葉片上掉
落的白霜與雪花，像一波波的浪花。

「她總是那麼纖細，弱不禁風，」精靈說，「但她卻有
顆寬闊的心！」

「你說得沒錯，」史顧己叫道：「她的確是這樣。我無
法否認，否則老天不會饒過我的！」

「她結婚後才去世的，」精靈說，「而且我記得她有小
孩。」

「一個孩子。」史顧己回答。

「沒錯，」精靈說，「你的外甥！」

第一個精靈

史顧己心頭有點不安，他簡短地答道：「嗯。」

儘管他們才離開學校沒多久，但很快地就來到了忙碌熱鬧的城市大街，街上滿是熙來攘往的人群，及爭相搶路的手推車與馬車，呈現出一個真實城市會有的喧囂紛擾。透過店鋪的裝飾，人們可以輕易看到，又是聖誕節了。現在已是傍晚時分，街上燈火通明。

精靈停在一間商店門前，問史顧己是否認得這間店。

「我知道！」史顧己說：「我過去不就是在這裡當學徒的嗎？」

他們走進店內，看見一位帶著威爾斯假髮的老先生，正坐在一張很高的桌子後方，要是他再高個兩吋，頭一定會撞上天花板的。史顧己興奮地尖叫：「天啊，那是老費茲維格呢！老天保佑，他復活了！」

老費茲維格放下筆，望了望時鐘，鐘指著七點。他搓搓手，整整寬大的背心，縱聲大笑，從頭到腳都很愉快的樣子。接著他發出愉悅開心、快活響亮的聲音叫道：「喲荷，好啦！埃比尼澤！狄克！」

過去的史顧己已經變成了年輕小伙子，他和另一名學徒很快地走進來。

「我確定那是狄克・威爾金斯！」史顧己向精靈說道，「天啊，就是他。他跟我很要好呢，這個狄克。可憐的狄克！親愛的，我親愛的啊！」

「嘿，我的孩子們，」費茲維格說道，「今晚不必工作了。狄克、埃比尼澤，今晚是聖誕夜呀，我們要過聖誕囉！
我們套上門板，停止營業吧。」老費茲維格雙手奮力一拍，
叫著：「馬上行動！」

你絕不會相信那兩個傢伙動作有多麼迅速！他們扛著門
板跑到街上——一、二、三——定位——四、五、六——閂
上門板、釘上門釘——七、八、九——你還沒數到十二之
前，他們就氣喘如牛地跑回來了。

「嘿！」老費茲維格喊著，異常靈活地從高桌子上跳下
來，「孩子們，我們把這裡收拾乾淨，挪出空間來！嘿，狄
克！哈，埃比尼澤！」

收拾乾淨！在老費茲維格的監督下，他們將所有東西清
理得乾乾淨淨。一分鐘內就收拾完畢。每一樣搬得開的東西
都移走了，彷彿這些東西已自大眾的生活中消失；地板洗刷
過了，燈芯修剪好了，火爐裡也堆上了煤；現在，整間店看
來就像一間整齊、溫暖、乾燥舒適且明亮的舞廳，讓人在寒
冷的冬天夜晚渴望入內。

一個帶著樂譜的小提琴手來了，他站上高高的桌子，將
那兒當成演奏席，並開始調音，但聽來卻像肚子絞痛的人所
發出的呻吟聲；隨後進來的是費茲維格太太，她的臉上帶著
開懷的笑容；三位愉快可人的費茲維格小姐也來了，後面跟
了六位為她們心碎的小伙子；店裡的年輕男女員工都來了；
費茲維格家的女傭和她當麵包師的表哥也來了；女廚子與她
哥哥的好友——擠乳男工——也進來了；還有對街的男孩也

來了，大家總懷疑他的主人沒有給他足夠的伙食，只見他躲在鄰家女孩的身後，女孩則是隔壁第二家的，老被女主人揪耳朵。他們一個個接踵而來；有的人含羞帶怯，有的人大大方方，有的表現優雅，有的看來笨拙，有的精力充沛，有的拖拖拉拉；不過無論如何，大家都來了。二十對佳偶全下場跳起舞來；他們手拉手繞了半圈又再繞回來，跳到中央然後又跳回原點；他們快快樂樂地交換了好幾次舞伴，又轉了好幾圈舞。原先領頭的一對搭檔總是跳錯位置，後來新的搭檔一到最前面時，就很快地重新起舞；到最後，大家都變成了領頭的搭檔，後面都沒有人。老費茲維格看到這樣的情形，拍著手叫道：「跳得好呀！」小提琴手則將他燙熱的臉埋進黑啤酒壺裡，這壺酒正是為此而專門預備的。但是他一抬頭，即使場內沒有舞者，他仍舊重新拉奏起來，好似原本那位筋疲力盡的小提琴手已被人用門板抬回家，他現在是一個全新的小提琴手，決心不成功便成仁。

　　他們又跳了幾支舞，玩了幾個處罰遊戲，再跳幾支舞，然後便開始享用聖誕大餐：有蛋糕、尼格斯酒、一大塊烤肉冷盤、一大塊水煮肉冷盤、碎肉餡餅，還有喝不完的啤酒。但是，在烤肉與水煮肉冷盤上來後，小提琴手（這傢伙精明得很！他很清楚自己該怎麼做，無須我們多言！）開始拉奏起「卡弗利爵士」舞曲，當晚的壓軸好戲才真正上場。費茲維格先生起身與費茲維格太太共舞，當領頭的一對，這可不是件簡單的任務；他們身後跟了二十三、四對的搭檔，全是不容小覷之輩，他們是來跳舞，不是來散步的。

　　但是就算再多上兩倍的人，不，應該說是四倍，老費茲維格還是能夠應付得宜，費茲維格太太亦不例外。說到老費茲維格太太，她在各方面都能夠與老費茲維格搭配。假如這讚美還不夠好，請告訴我還有什麼更棒的讚美，好讓我立刻採用。老費茲維格的小腿肚上似乎放射出一道耀眼的光芒，彷彿月光般地照亮每個舞步。無論何時，你都猜不透他們下一個舞步究竟是什麼。老費茲維格與太太跳完所有的舞步：前進後退、舞伴牽手、鞠躬屈膝、迴旋、雙手環繞、回到原位；老費茲維格最後還一躍而起，雙腿在空中交叉，他的動作靈巧，速度快得像眨眼似的，最後穩穩地落地，晃也沒晃。

　　鐘聲敲響十一下時，室內的舞會便結束了。費茲維格夫婦各站在門的一邊，與每個離去的客人握手，並祝賀他們聖誕快樂。即使屋內最後只剩下兩個學徒，他們也同樣跟學徒握手祝賀。於是，快樂的喧鬧聲漸漸遠去，兩個小夥子也回到店後面櫃檯底下的床上睡覺了。

　　在這期間，史顧己就像個失魂落魄的人。他的心神都飛到那個場景裡，回到了往日的自己。他認出這一切，憶起這一切，享受這一切，他激動萬分。一直到了年少的史顧己與狄克那發亮的臉龐轉了過去，史顧己才想起精靈正在身旁，並警覺到它正望著他，而它頭上的那道光束變得更為亮眼了。

第一個精靈

「一件小事就能讓這些傻瓜感激不盡。」精靈說道。

「小事?」史顧己應道。

精靈示意他注意聽那兩個學徒的對話,他們衷心地讚美費茲維格。史顧己聽完後,精靈說:「天啊!難道不是這樣嗎?費茲維格只不過花了幾磅錢,大概三或四磅吧,這就值得你們大力吹捧嗎?」

「並不是這樣的。」史顧己激動地回答,說話的樣子不自覺地又回到年少的模樣,而非現在的他,「精靈,話不能這麼說。他有能力決定讓我們快不快樂,讓我們的工作輕鬆或沉重,是樂趣或苦役。就算他只是以言語、臉色或一些微不足道的小事來行使這份能力,那又如何呢?他帶給我們的快樂卻如一大筆的財富哪。」

他察覺到精靈正在看他,於是停了下來。

「怎麼了?」精靈問道。

「沒什麼。」史顧己回答。

「我知道有事。」精靈堅持說。

「不,」史顧己說,「沒什麼。只是,我想到剛才應該跟我的員工說一兩句話,就這樣。」

此時,年少的史顧己已祈禱完,熄了燈;史顧己與鬼魂再度肩並肩地站在外頭的街上。

「我的時間不多了,快點!」精靈說。

這話並不是對著史顧己或身旁任何人說的,但卻隨即起了效果。因為史顧己再次看見過去的自己——年紀大了些,變成了一個青年。那張臉上還沒有日後幾年的尖銳嚴酷，卻開始有了煩惱與貪婪的神色。他的眼神閃動著焦急、貪昧與不耐，顯示他心中有一股狂熱已生根，而它長出來的大樹已在那雙眸中投下了陰影。

青年史顧已並不是獨自一人，身旁還坐著一位穿著喪服的美麗少女。少女的眼眶盈滿淚水，在聖誕精靈的光芒照射下閃閃發光。

「這沒什麼。」女孩柔聲說道，「對你來說，這根本沒什麼。你心中已有另一個偶像取代了我；要是那個偶像能夠像我過去一樣，試圖努力地取悅安慰你，那我也沒什麼好悲傷難過的。」

「誰取代妳了？」他反問。

「一個黃金偶像。」

「這個世界可真是公平啊！」他說，「人生最難挨的是貧窮，但追求財富卻又得遭到最嚴厲的譴責！」

「你太恐懼這個世界了，」她溫柔地答道，「你把所有的願望都放在追求財富，就是不要因貧窮而受人恥笑。我眼看你崇高的抱負一個接一個地破滅，最後只剩下一個主要的慾望：財富。不是嗎？」

「那又怎麼樣？」他反駁道，「假如我變聰明了，那又怎麼樣？我對妳始終不變。」

她搖搖頭。

「我變了嗎？」

第一個精靈

　　「我們的婚約是過去立下的。當時我們都很窮困，卻對一切心滿意足，只期待有一天能夠靠著耐心勤勉來改善我們的經濟狀況。但你現在變了，你已不是當初立下婚約時的那個人了。」

　　「我那時只是個孩子。」他煩躁地說。

　　「你心裡明白，你再也不是過去的你，」她回嘴，「我卻沒變。當初我們心靈合一時帶給我們幸福的泉源，現在卻成了我們貌合神離時的痛苦根源。我有多常想到這一點，心又有多痛，就不用多說了。重點是我已注意到這一點，並願意讓你離去。」

　　「我曾說過要離妳而去嗎？」

　　「口頭上沒有，你從未說過。」

　　「那我又是怎麼表達的？」

　　「從你所改變的特質、個性、生活環境、人生目標，還有那些過去會讓你重視我情意的一切。假如我們之間沒有這紙婚約，」女孩望著他，神色溫和卻相當堅定，「告訴我，你現在還會找我出來，試圖贏得我的心嗎？噢，你不會的！」

　　史顧己似乎不由自主地承認了這段話，但他心頭掙扎了一下，還是說道：「妳錯了。」

　　「如果可以的話，我也希望是我想錯了。」她回答，「天知道！要我接受這樣的事實，要有多麼強大不可避免的理由呢。假如今天、明天或昨天的你都能夠自由選擇，我能相信你會選擇一個沒有嫁妝的女孩嗎？你對這個女孩所說的每句話，不都是以利益來衡量的嗎？你只是一時昏了頭選擇她，我難道不清楚你將來一定會懊悔嗎？我知道會這樣子，所以我讓你解脫。我全心全意地愛著過去的你。」

他正準備開口，不料她卻掉頭繼續說：「你或許對此感到痛苦，我們過去的回憶也讓我希望你會。不過，很快你就會忘得一乾二淨，就好像慶幸自己及時從一個無利可圖的夢中醒過來一樣。願你在自己選擇的人生裡活得快樂。」

她離開了他，他們分手了。

「精靈，」史顧己說道，「別再讓我看下去了！讓我回家。你為什麼要折磨我？」

「再看一幕幻影吧！」精靈喊道。

「不要了！」史顧己大叫，「不要再看了，我不想看！別讓我看了！」

但是殘酷的精靈挾著他的雙手，強迫他繼續看下一幕。

他們又置身於另一個場景：一間不是很輝煌華麗，但卻很舒適的房間。溫暖的爐火邊，坐著一位美麗的少女，她跟史顧己剛剛看到的那位女子非常相像，他原本以為是同一人，直到又看見坐在她對面的「她」，才知道美麗的她已嫁為人婦，這年輕的女孩是她的女兒。房間裡的喧嘩聲驚天動地，因為裡面有許多小孩，多到讓心情激動的史顧已數也數不清；這跟某首詩裡所形容的「四十隻牛吃草時，寂靜無聲，好像只有一隻」不同，眼前的四十個孩子可不像只有一個人，相反的，每個人倒像又多了四十個化身。整間屋子哄鬧得不得了，但沒有人在意。那對母女反而笑得樂不可支呢，似乎很享受這種感覺。不久，那個女兒也加入這些小孩子，卻慘遭那些小土匪們最無情的攻擊。啊，若我能加入他們，我願意付出任何代價！但是我不會這麼地粗魯，不會，絕不會！即使給我全世界的財富，我也不會拉扯那女孩的髮辮讓它散落，也不會剝掉那可愛的小鞋子，我以性命對天發誓！至於像那些小孩子這樣測量她的腰圍，即使我是個大膽的年輕小伙子，我也不敢如此，我怕上帝會懲罰我，讓我的胳臂彎成環腰的形狀，再也伸不直。但是，我真的渴望能夠觸碰她的櫻桃小嘴；我想問她一個問題，讓她不得不輕啟朱唇回答；我想迎向她低垂的睫毛，讓她的臉因發窘而泛紅；我想讓她放下一頭波浪般的秀髮，那每一吋髮絲都是無價的紀念——總之，我得承認，我多麼想要能夠像個孩子般肆無忌憚，卻又成熟得足以明瞭這份價值。

　　此刻，門上傳來一陣敲門聲。笑臉盈盈、衣裳凌亂的女孩立刻被這群臉蛋紅撲撲的吵鬧小鬼頭簇擁到門前，好迎接他們的父親，他旁邊還跟著一個提滿聖誕禮物及玩具的送貨

員。在一陣尖叫及爭吵聲中,這毫無招架之力的可憐送貨員
慘遭猛烈攻擊!這群孩子拿椅子當梯子,搜探他的口袋,搶
走所有棕色紙盒,並緊緊捉住他的圍巾,雙手纏著他的脖
子,小小的手捶著他的背,還直踢著他的腳。他們每拆開一
個禮物,就發出驚奇快樂的尖叫聲。突然一聲恐怖的驚叫響
起,因為小嬰兒正要將洋娃娃的煎鍋塞入嘴巴裡,而且他們
懷疑他已經吞下一隻黏在大淺盤上的假火雞了。還好,他們
找到了那隻火雞,大夥才鬆了一口氣。他們的歡樂、感激、
狂喜都是難以言喻的!這群小孩子最後終於帶著激昂的情緒
離開客廳,上了樓梯,回到屋子頂樓,然後上床,一切才回
復平靜。

　　史顧己現在更專注看著眼前的景象:屋子的主人走到火
爐旁,在妻子身邊坐了下來,他的女兒惹人憐愛地倚在他的
腳旁;當史顧己想到,這優雅又前程似錦的女孩原本有可能
是自己的女兒,為自己人生的酷寒帶來暖春時,他的眼角就
濕了起來。

　　「貝拉,」丈夫微笑地轉向妻子說道,「我今天下午看
到妳的一位老朋友。」

　　「誰啊?」

　　「猜猜看。」

　　「我怎麼猜得著呢?呃,難不成⋯⋯」她跟丈夫一起笑
了起來,「是史顧己先生嗎?」

　　「正是。我從他辦公室的窗前經過;當時窗子沒關,他

點了根蠟燭在裡頭，我忍不住朝裡頭望。我聽說他的夥伴快死了，所以他一個人坐在那裡。我想他一定非常孤單。」

「精靈，」史顧已以哽咽的聲音說道，「帶我離開。」

「我告訴過你，這是過去的幻影。」精靈說道，「事實就是如此，別怨我！」

「帶我離開！」史顧已大吼，「我受不了了！」

他轉向精靈，發現那張正望著他的臉變得非常奇怪，剛才它讓他看到的所有臉孔，都有一小部份出現在他的臉上。他衝上前捉住它。

「你走開！帶我回去。別再捉弄我了！」

在一陣掙扎之後——如果這可以稱為掙扎的話，因為精靈這邊顯然沒有任何抵抗，且對於對手的力量也沒有任何反應——史顧已看到精靈所散發出的光芒越來越明亮。他隱約覺得這道光與精靈的影響力有關，於是他捉住那頂滅光帽，突然就朝精靈頭頂蓋上去。

精靈因而縮了下去，滅光帽蓋住了整個身體；不過，即使史顧已使盡了全力壓著帽子，也無法掩蓋滅光帽下流洩出來的光芒，光芒蔓延了整個地面。

史顧已感到筋疲力竭且充滿睡意。接著，他發現自己回到了房間。他又壓了帽子一下才鬆手，然後跌跌撞撞地走到床邊，一倒下便睡著了。

第三樂章
第二個精靈

　　史顧己在濃濃的鼾聲中醒了過來，他坐起身來，整理一下思緒。無須任何人的提醒他就知道，一點鐘的鐘聲又快響了。他覺得自己清醒得正是時候，正好可以和雅各‧馬利所安排的第二位精靈談談。但是，史顧己一猜起這位新來的精靈會拉開哪邊的床帷時，卻覺得全身發冷很不舒服。於是，他自己動手將周圍的床帷都給拉開，然後重新躺下，嚴密地監視四周。他希望能夠在精靈出現時就做好準備，而不要又因驚嚇而表現得緊張無措。

　　那些不拘小節的紳士們總是裝出經歷過大風大浪又世故的模樣，他們誇耀自己從拋錢遊戲到殺人都很在行，好表現出自己能力非凡的樣子。當然，在擲錢遊戲和殺人這兩個極端之間，有其他林林總總的事情。我不敢說史顧己有多厲害，但我要讓各位知道，他已經做好心理準備，預備面對任何奇怪的東西，無論即將出現的是嬰兒或是犀牛，他都不會被嚇到了。

　　現在，他已經準備好要面對任何東西了，不料四下卻毫無動靜。最後，當鐘聲敲了一下，卻沒有任何東西出現時，他渾身顫慄。五分鐘，十分鐘，十五分鐘過去了，仍然毫無動靜。這期間他躺在床上，四周籠罩著紅色的光芒——這道光是一點的鐘聲響起時蔓延進來的。這一道光芒比十二個鬼魂更讓史顧己驚慌，因為他不知道它代表什麼意思，或是預示了什麼。有幾次他都擔心，他有可能在一瞬間起火燃燒，自己卻渾然不知。然而，最後他終於想到——正如你我一開始就想到的，因為旁觀者總是知道應該怎麼做，且早就採取行動了——我剛剛說了，最後他終於想到這道光可能來自隔壁房間；他更進一步地望著那道光時，發現它的確是從隔壁房裡流洩出來的。這想法佔據了他的心，他緩緩下床，穿著拖鞋走到鄰房門口。

史顧己的手才剛放到門把上，就有一個奇怪的聲音喊出他的名字，並命令他進去。他乖乖遵從了。

這是史顧己的房間，一個毋庸置疑的事實。但是，這房間顯然大大變了樣：牆壁和天花板上都懸掛著綠葉，使得房間看來像極了小叢林，且到處都有色澤鮮豔的漿果閃閃發光；冬青樹、槲寄生及常春藤青綠的葉子反射著亮光，恍若四下散置了許多小鏡子；壁爐內熊熊的火焰竄起，衝向煙囪。在史顧己居住這裡的期間，或者是馬利的時代，或者是過去好幾個冬季裡，這可是從來沒有過的景象；地板上成堆的食物高聳得像個王座，有火雞、鵝肉、野味、雞鴨、肉凍、大肉塊、乳豬、成串的香腸、碎肉餅、葡萄乾布丁、一桶桶的牡蠣、熱騰騰的栗子、鮮紅的蘋果、多汁的柳橙、甘甜的鮮梨、二十吋的大蛋糕，還有酒桶內流動不停的潘趣

第二個精靈

酒，種種美味的食物和令人垂涎的熱氣讓小房間裡煙霧瀰漫。在這舒適的王座上，坐著一個興高采烈的巨人，畫面看來頗為壯觀。巨人手裡握著一把形狀很像「豐饒之角」的火把，當史顧己在門邊偷窺時，它便高舉火把，將光照亮在史顧己身上。

「進來吧！」精靈叫道，「進來吧！這樣你才能更了解我啊，老兄！」

史顧己怯生生地走了進來，低垂著頭站在精靈面前。他不再是過去那個頑強的史顧己了，儘管精靈的雙眼澄澈和藹，他還是不想與它對視。

「我是現在的耶誕精靈，」精靈說道，「抬頭看看我！」

史顧己恭恭敬敬地照辦了。這個精靈穿著一件簡單的綠色長袍，或者也可以說是斗篷，滾邊飾滿了白色的羽毛。衣服寬鬆地穿在巨人身上，他巨大的胸膛都露了出來，像是討厭用任何東西加以保護或遮掩。繁複的衣褶下露出一雙赤裸裸的腳，而它的頭上則戴了一頂冬青花環，花環上散插著幾根發亮的小冰柱。巨人長長的棕色捲髮隨意地披著，就跟它那快活的臉龐、閃爍的雙眼、敞開的雙手、愉悅的聲音、怡然的態度及歡樂的神情一樣隨意自在。它的腰際上繫著一個古式劍鞘，不過裡頭並沒有劍，而且那古式的劍鞘也都鏽跡斑斑了。

「你從未見過像我這樣的吧！」精靈大聲問道。

「從來沒有。」史顧己回答。

「你也從未碰過我家裡的其他年輕成員吧？我指的是我那些這幾年才出生的哥哥們（因為我還很年輕）。」精靈繼續追問。

「恐怕沒有。」史顧己回答，「精靈，你有很多的兄弟嗎？」

「超過一千八百個呢！」精靈說道。

「還真是好大一個嗷嗷待哺的家庭啊！」史顧己咕噥道。

現在的耶誕精靈站起身來。

「精靈，」史顧己柔順地說，「請帶我到任何你要去的地方。昨晚我雖是受到逼迫，但也上了一課，受益良多。今晚，假如你要教導我，我也希望能有所獲。」

「摸我的袍子。」史顧己聽從精靈的話，牢牢地捉住長袍。

瞬間，房裡的冬青、檞寄生、紅漿果、常春藤、火雞、鵝肉、野味、雞鴨、肉凍、肉塊、乳豬、香腸、牡蠣、派、布丁、水果及潘趣酒都消失了。房間、爐火、紅色的光芒及夜晚也都不見了。此刻，他們已站在聖誕節早晨的市區街道上，在那裡（因為當時天氣嚴寒），人們都忙著剷除門前人行道上及屋頂上的冰雪，並一同發出了清脆悅耳的聲音。小男孩們看到屋頂上的冰雪撲通地掉落到地面的街道，飛散成小型的人造暴風雪時，個個都樂壞了。

第二個精靈

　　和覆蓋在屋頂上的皚皚白雪相比，或與地面上髒汙的雪相較，房子的門面看來真夠黑的了，而窗戶居然更黑。地面上的積雪有著手推車及馬車沉重的車痕，在街道的交岔口地段，車痕重疊數百次，形成了複雜的溝渠，但在濃厚的黃泥漿及冰水的覆蓋下，已難以辨識。天色陰霾，半融半凝的霧氣籠罩著街道，較重的霧氣粒子隨著煤炭原子落下，好似全大不列顛的煙囪說好了一起燃火，盡情燃燒。這天氣或城鎮並沒有特別令人愉快的事物，但空氣裡卻有股歡樂的氣氛，這是最清爽的夏季氣息或最明亮的夏陽也無法製造的。

　　在屋頂上鏟雪的人們都非常地快活歡樂，他們隔著低矮的擋牆互相叫喚，現在還開玩笑地互丟起雪球來了——這些大自然的飛彈比任何口頭玩笑好得多——假如他們擊中對方便哈哈大笑，就算沒中，他們也一樣開心。家禽店的鋪子仍半掩著門，水果店看來依然琳瑯滿目：裝滿栗子的大籃子圓滾滾的，像樂陶陶的老紳士們穿著背心靠在門邊，那肥墩墩的大肚子都凸到街上了；紅皮、棕臉且粗腰的西班牙洋蔥，活像是豐腴的西班牙修道士，在架上不斷朝著經過的女孩放縱且俏皮地眨眼，但一瞄到牆上懸掛的槲寄生時，眼神便又端莊起來；梨子與蘋果則堆得高高的，像座金字塔；託店家的福，成串的葡萄掛在很顯眼的地方，讓過往的行人都不由自主地流下口水；一堆長滿絨毛的褐色榛子所散發出的芳香，不禁令人憶起林間的古老小徑，以及涉過深及足踝的枯葉的樂趣；矮矮胖胖的暗紅色諾克福蘋果，在鮮黃的柳橙與

檸檬間看來格外耀眼，它們挺著多汁的結實身軀，急切地乞求路人用紙袋將它們帶回家，在晚餐後享用；各式各樣的水果中，擺置著一只魚缸，裡頭有幾隻金色、銀色的魚兒，牠們雖然遲鈍又冷血，但也知道今天有點特別，所以，帶著懶洋洋的熱情，緩緩地在自己的小世界裡悠遊著。

雜貨店啊！噢，雜貨店啊！幾近關門狀態的店鋪，大概只有一兩片門板未蓋上，但從縫隙中還是可以見到這樣的景象：櫃檯上的秤盤發出了歡樂的聲響；捲軸將細繩清脆地切斷；金屬罐子像搖鈴般上下晃動響鬧著；茶葉與咖啡混合成一種誘人的香味；葡萄乾又多又罕見；杏仁純白；肉桂棒又直又長，其他的香料可口美味；糖漬水果上裹著化掉的糖衣，讓最不受誘惑的人看了也會為之暈眩；無花果濕潤多汁；法國的酸李在高級的包裝盒內散發出微紅的色澤；每件有關聖誕節包裝的東西看起來都非常可口；而在今天這個充滿希望的日子裡，顧客們都顯得匆匆忙忙，以致於他們在門邊撞成一團，粗魯地撞壞了購物籃，或者把購買的東西忘在櫃檯上，只好又返身回來，類似的錯誤重複了幾百次，但他們還是保持著絕佳的心情；雜貨店老闆與員工更是熱誠親切，繫在他們圍裙後面閃閃發亮的金屬心別針，就好像是他們自己的心一樣，他們將它掏出來供大家觀看，就算聖誕節的寒鴉想要啄一啄也歡迎。

不久，教堂尖塔的鐘聲開始呼喚老百姓到教堂與禮拜堂去，於是大家穿上最好的衣裳，臉上帶著最愉快的神情走往

教堂。同時，無以計數的人們從街道巷弄和許多不知名的轉
角處湧出，帶著晚餐來到麵包店。看到這麼多準備參加宴會
的貧窮人，精靈似乎感到很有趣，它和史顧己一起站在麵包
店的門口，只要有人捧著晚餐經過，它便掀開飯盒的蓋子，
在他們的食物上灑下一點火把的香灰。這把火炬非常特殊，
只要一有人互帶怒氣地推擠對方，精靈只需從火把上撒下幾
滴水到他們身上，這些人便立刻又恢復了風度。就如他們所
說的，在耶誕節吵架實在是一種羞恥。可不是嗎！上帝有
眼，可不是嗎！

　　鐘聲停止時，麵包鋪的門也關上了。不過，晚餐和烹飪
都已經開始快樂地進行，每個麵包店火爐上的雪都開始融
化，就連人行道上也冒著騰騰熱氣，猶如人行道鋪石也正在
烹調食物呢。

　　「你火把上灑下來的東西有特別的味道吧？」史顧己問
道。

　　「是的，一種屬於我自己的味道。」

　　「它可以撒在各種聖誕節晚餐裡嗎？」史顧己又問。

　　「任何一種晚餐都適用，窮人的晚餐尤能發揮作用。」

　　「為何對窮人的晚餐更能發揮作用呢？」史顧己問。

　　「因為他們最需要它。」

　　「精靈，」史顧己沉思了一會兒說道，「我真好奇，為
何在我們周遭各界中，只有你想要約束這些窮人，剝奪他們
純真歡樂的機會。」

第二個精靈

「我？」精靈尖叫。

「你每隔七天就要剝奪他們用餐的機會，這一天通常是他們能夠好好用上一餐的日子，」史顧己說，「不是嗎？」

「我？」精靈大嚷。

「你企圖讓麵包鋪在禮拜日關門，不是嗎？」史顧己說，「結果就是這樣。」

「我？」精靈喊道。

「假如我說錯了，那很抱歉。不過，禮拜天休息是假借你的名義，或至少是依你家族成員的名義所造成的。」

「在你們的地球上，」精靈回答：「有些人宣稱認識我們，並假借我們的名義，進行各種狂熱、驕傲、陰險、仇恨、嫉妒、偏見或自私的行為。其實我們根本不認識這些人，就好像他們不曾存在過似的。記住這一點，他們要為自己的行為負責，別把他們的帳算在我們頭上。」

史顧己答應了。隨即，他們就跟之前一樣，隱身來到市郊。精靈有一種特異的能力（史顧己在麵包鋪就發現了）：儘管它身型龐大，但在任何地方都能夠很輕易地安身；即使現在站在低矮的屋簷下，它還是展現出精靈的優雅氣質，恍若自己身處輝煌的大廳一樣。

或許是這位善良的精靈樂於展現自己這份能力，也或許是因為它對窮人都有著和善、慷慨、悲天憫人的特質及同情心，它直接找上了史顧己的職員。它要史顧己捉著長袍，然後便帶史顧己來到職員的家門前。精靈微笑地停在門檻上，並以火把灑下他對這家人的祝福。想想看！鮑勃一個禮拜不過賺十五先令，每個禮拜六口袋裡也只會有十五個銅板，但現在耶誕精靈竟然降福在他這間只有四個房間的小屋子。

這時，克勞契太太——也就是鮑勃的妻子——站起身來，她為了今天特別打扮一番，但穿的只不過就是一件翻改了兩次的禮服，上面繫滿了緞帶；這些便宜的緞帶只花了六便士，但卻發揮了很大的作用。她鋪上桌巾，二女兒貝琳達在一旁幫忙，身穿的禮服也繫滿了緞帶。長子彼得克勞契正把叉子叉入裝滿馬鈴薯的長柄鍋裡，並一邊咬著身上過大襯衫的衣領角（這衣服是鮑勃的財產，但在這個特別的日子裡，他將衣服送給了兒子兼繼承人），他很高興自己可以穿得如此時髦，甚至渴望能到公園秀一秀。此時，兩個較年幼的孩子衝了進來，一男一女，嘴裡嚷著，他們在麵包鋪的外面就聞到了鵝肉的味道，而且他們知道這是從家裡傳出來的。一想到鼠尾草與洋蔥的香味，兩個年幼的孩子就高興得圍著餐桌跳舞，並將彼得捧上了天，此時他（雖然被衣領勒得快窒息了，卻還是一副若無其事的樣子，）正搧著爐火，直到慢性子的馬鈴薯終於煮熟，在長柄鍋裡吵鬧地敲打鍋蓋，希望有人趕快釋放它們，並撕下它們的皮。

「你們的寶貝父親呢？」克勞契太太說道，「還有你們的弟弟小提姆呢？還有瑪莎呢？去年的聖誕節她可沒遲到半個鐘頭呢！」

「媽媽，瑪莎在這兒！」一個女孩出現了。

　「媽媽，瑪莎在這兒！」
兩個年幼的孩子喊道，「呀荷，
瑪莎，我們有一隻鵝呢！」

　「天啊，親愛的，妳遲到好
久了！」克勞契太太說著，親
吻了女孩好幾下，隨即就熱心
地替她取下圍巾與帽子。

　「媽媽，我們昨晚有好多
工作要做，」女孩回答，「而且
今早又得收拾乾淨！」

　「好，好！沒人怪妳這麼晚才回來，」克勞契太太說
道：「到爐火旁坐下，取取暖，上帝保佑妳，親愛的！」

　「不，不！爸爸回來了，」兩個年幼的孩子跑來跑去
地嚷著，「躲起來，瑪莎，躲起來！」

　於是瑪莎便躲了起來。小鮑勃進來了，他身前披著的
圍巾至少有三呎長，而身上破舊的衣服已經縫補刷平過了，
以便有個過節的樣子，他的肩上還扛著小提姆。可憐的小提
姆握著一根小枴杖，兩隻腳上還裝著支撐用的金屬架。

「天啊，瑪莎呢？」鮑勃克勞契環顧四周，尖叫地問。

「沒回來。」克勞契夫人回答。

「沒回來！」才剛扛著小提姆從教堂衝回家的鮑勃忽然洩了氣似地說：「聖誕節竟然不回家！」

瑪莎不喜歡看見父親失望，即便只是玩笑，所以她從剛剛躲藏的櫥櫃門後走了出來，撲進父親的懷中，而兩個年幼的孩子則簇擁著小提姆走到洗衣房，因為從那裡才能聽到布丁在鍋裡嘶嘶作響的聲音。

「提姆表現得如何？」鮑勃開心地摟著女兒時，克勞契夫人挪揄了他一陣後問道。

「好得不得了，」鮑勃說，「甚至還要更好呢。怪的是，他總是一個人坐著沉思，想些妳從未聽過的稀奇古怪的事情。在回家的路上他告訴我，希望教堂的人都能看看他，因為他雙腳殘廢，看到他會讓大家在耶誕節這天想起，耶穌曾讓跛腳的人走路、讓盲眼的人重見光明，他覺得這會很令人開心的。」

鮑勃說這段話時聲音微微地顫抖；繼而說道小提姆越來越堅強善良時，抖得更為厲害。

在他們還沒說出其他話前，地板便傳來活動枴杖的聲響，小提姆回來了；他的哥哥姊姊在一旁攙著他，將他扶到火爐旁的小凳子上。鮑勃則挽起袖口——可憐的傢伙，這袖子簡直破爛到不行——調製一種混合熱飲，在水壺裡放入了杜松子酒及檸檬，一遍遍地攪拌後，再將水壺放到鍋架上以火慢燉。長子彼得和那兩個到處亂跑的弟妹去端鵝肉，一會兒便浩浩蕩蕩地回來了。

他們所引起的騷動，會讓你以為鵝是世上最珍奇的鳥類，連黑天鵝也望塵莫及——在這個家裡，這或許是個事實。克勞契太太正將事先已裝在小長柄鍋裡的肉汁加熱，長子彼得以充沛的精力搗碎馬鈴薯，貝琳達在蘋果醬中加糖，瑪莎擦拭熱盤子，鮑勃帶著小提姆坐在桌子一角，另外兩個年幼的孩子為大家擺放椅子，當然也忘不了他們自己的，然後他們爬上椅子，把湯匙塞到嘴巴裡，免得因為等不及要吃鵝肉而尖叫。最後，菜餚終於就緒，飯前禱告也結束了。克勞契太太不慌不忙地望向切肉刀，準備拿起它切鵝胸時，全場一陣屏息。當她終於一刀劃下，而大家期望已久的 餡露了出來時，餐桌旁不禁響起愉悅的低聲歡呼，即使是小提姆，也受到兩個年幼孩子的影響，興奮地拿著刀敲打餐桌，並以虛弱的聲音歡呼。

這隻鵝真是史無前例。鮑勃說他從未看過這樣的烤鵝。那柔軟香甜的肉質、龐大的體積及便宜的價格獲得了大家一致的讚賞。再加上蘋果醬與馬鈴薯泥，對這個家庭而言，這實在是太豐盛了；正如克勞契太太高興地宣布的（在檢查過了盤子裡的一小塊骨頭肉後），鵝肉還有剩呢！每個人都吃得很撐，尤其是兩個年幼的孩子，連眉毛都沾上了鼠尾草與洋蔥醬汁。此時，貝琳達小姐開始換盤子，而克勞契太太獨自離開房間——她太緊張了，所以不想讓人跟隨——去將布丁起鍋，然後端上桌。

　　想想看，萬一布丁沒有熟呢？想想看，萬一布丁一拿出來就裂開了呢？想想看，萬一有人在他們享用鵝肉時，從後院翻牆而入，偷拿走布丁了呢？這些想法令兩個年幼的孩子極度不安，他們的腦海中假想著各種可怕的畫面。

　　萬歲！一股熱騰騰的蒸氣湧上來了！布丁出爐了。聞起來有著洗衣日的氣味，那是裹在外頭那塊布的味道。另外，還有餐館的味道，是一家緊臨著糕餅鋪與洗衣房的氣味！那就是布丁的味道。半分鐘之後，克勞契太太進來了，她的臉泛紅，得意地笑著，手裡端著的布丁宛若布滿斑點的砲彈，既緊密又紮實，周圍還有四分之一品脫的白蘭地酒正熊熊地燃燒著，上頭則插著聖誕冬青的枝葉作為裝飾。

　　噢，多麼棒的一個布丁啊！鮑勃克勞契冷靜地說，他覺得這是自他們結婚以來，克勞契太太最偉大的成就。克勞契太太則說，既然現在已鬆了一口氣，她得承認起初還有點擔心麵粉的份量不對。每個人都想發表意見，但絕對沒有半個人會說或會想到，這個布丁其實對這麼一大家子來說實在太小了——要是有人這麼做簡直不可原諒。任何一個克勞契家的成員都不會厚著臉皮說出這樣的話。

　　最後，晚餐結束了，桌巾也收拾了，火爐也打掃了，火焰重新燃燒起來。水壺裡的混合飲料嚐起來非常地美味，蘋果與柳橙擺上了桌，還有一鏟子滿滿的栗子正放在爐火上烤呢。克勞契一家人圍坐在火爐旁——鮑勃克勞契稱之為一個

圓，但其實只是半圓。鮑勃的手邊排放著家裡所有的玻璃杯：兩個大玻璃杯，以及一個沒有把手的果凍杯。

　　無論如何，用這些杯子盛裝水壺裡的混合飲料，味道並不輸給高腳酒杯。鮑勃愉快地倒著熱飲時，爐火上的栗子開始劈里啪啦地裂開了。鮑勃接著舉杯宣布：「親愛的，祝我們大家聖誕快樂。願上帝祝福我們！」

　　全家人跟著他說了一遍。

　　「願上帝祝福我們每個人！」小提姆最後一個說。

　　小提姆坐在自己的小板凳上，跟父親靠得很近。鮑勃握住他瘦弱的小手，好像很愛這個孩子，希望能夠將他留在身邊，深怕有人把他帶走。

　　「精靈，」史顧己帶著前所未有的關懷之意說道，「告訴我，小提姆能夠存活下來嗎？」

　　「我在冷清的壁爐旁看到了一張空椅子，」精靈回答：「及一支受到珍藏的枴杖。假如這些幻影不變，這孩子將活不久。」

　　「不，不要，」史顧己說，「噢，不，善良的精靈！告訴我他會活著。」

　　「假如這些幻影未來也沒改變，那麼，」精靈回答道，「我們這些精靈就不會再在這裡看到他。那又有什麼關係呢？假如他得死掉，那就死了算了，這樣還可以緩解人口過剩的壓力。」

　　史顧己低下頭，聽著精靈引用他說過的話，心中悔恨萬千。

「人類，」精靈說，「假如你心中還有一點人性，不是那麼鐵石心腸的話，那在你真正了解人口過剩的意義，以及過剩的問題出在哪裡之前，就別再說那種缺德的鬼話。你可以決定誰該活，誰該死嗎？或許，從上帝的觀點來看，你比數百萬個貧窮人家的孩子更不值得也更沒資格活著。噢，上帝，聽聽看，葉子上的蟲正在大放厥詞，說牠在泥土裡挨餓的兄弟數量太多了！」

在精靈的譴責下，史顧己彎下身子，全身顫抖地凝視地面。但他驀然地又抬起眼，因為他聽到了自己的名字。

「史顧己先生！」鮑勃說道，「我們來敬史顧己先生，他是讓我們擁有這頓大餐的恩人呢！」

「的確，他是讓我們擁有這頓大餐的恩人！」克勞契太太漲紅著臉叫道，「我真希望他在這兒。那我就可以將心掏出來給他享用，希望他吃得下去。」

「親愛的，」鮑勃說，「孩子在這兒，何況，今天是聖誕節呢。」

「我當然知道今天是聖誕節，」她回答，「只有在這一天，我們才會為史顧己先生這麼可恨、吝嗇、冷血且鐵石心腸的人舉杯。你知道的，鮑勃！沒人比你更清楚他了，可憐的你！」

「親愛的，」鮑勃溫和地回答，「今天是聖誕節。」

「我可不是為了他，是看在你及聖誕節的份上，我才為他乾杯，」克勞契太太說道，「祝他長命百歲！聖誕快樂及新年快樂！……我敢肯定，他一定很高興、很愉快！」

孩子們跟著她乾杯——這是他們第一次那麼心不甘情不願。小提姆是最後一個乾杯的，但他半點興致都沒有。史顧己是這個家庭的惡魔，一提到他的名字，這歡樂的宴會便籠罩一層陰影，足足有五分鐘都消散不了。

這層陰影散去後，他們比之前歡樂十倍——光是驅散了史顧己這個邪惡的陰影，就夠他們安心了。鮑勃克勞契告訴他們，他替長子彼得留意了一份工作，如果談成的話，一個禮拜就能賺進五先令六便士。兩個年幼的孩子一想到彼得工作的模樣，就忍不住放聲大笑，而彼得凝視著爐火若有所思，彷彿正在斟酌，若有了一筆進帳應該從事何種投資。在女帽店當學徒的瑪莎，則告訴他們她的工作性質，以及她一口氣工作多少個小時，還說明早她可要好好地睡個懶覺了，因為她明天休假。另外，她也提到前些日子看到一位伯爵夫人與勛爵的事，她說伯爵與彼得一樣高，彼得因此拉高了衣領，讓人無法看見他的頭顱。這期間，栗子和熱飲傳了一圈又一圈。之後，小提姆為他們唱了一首歌，內容描述一個在雪地裡迷失方向的孩子；他的音量不大，略帶哀傷，卻唱得棒極了。

這個宴會並無特別出色之處。他們不是富有的人家，無法盛裝打扮，鞋子不能防水，衣服也不夠穿，而且彼得很可能也進過當鋪。但是，他們都非常快樂，充滿感恩，和樂融

第二個精靈

融，對聖誕節也很滿足。他們的身影漸漸淡去了，但在精靈臨去之際，用火炬所灑下明亮的火星前，他們看來更加愉悅歡快，史顧己一直看著他們，尤其是小提姆，直到他們完全消失。

此時，天色漸暗，雪積得更厚了。史顧己與精靈沿著街道前進時，家家戶戶的廚房、大廳及各個房間所映射出來的燈光看起來真是美極了。這一家燭光搖曳，顯然正忙著準備溫馨的晚餐，一道道美味的菜餚正在爐火前加熱，深紅色的窗帷也預備好要拉攏，將寒冷黑暗隔絕在外；那一家，所有的小孩都跑到屋外的雪地上，迎接已婚的兄姊、表哥、姑姑回家團聚，他們爭先恐後地搶當第一；另一家，賓客們的影子映上了窗戶；那頭，一群漂亮的女孩全都穿戴著頭巾與毛靴，嘰嘰喳喳地走向鄰近的房子，唉，那些單身漢眼睜睜地看著她們容光煥發地走進屋裡——這些迷人的女孩可精明得很，她們心裡對自己的魅力再清楚不過了。

但是，假如你看到路上趕往聚會的人數，可能會想，這些人到達目的地時，豈不沒人出來迎接他們了嗎？其實，每家人的爐火都竄得老高，好迎接客人。精靈看到這樣的畫面，開心得不得了，它露出寬闊的胸膛，張開巨大的手，飄在空中，在範圍可及之處，慷慨地灑下光明和快樂。一個點燈工人正為黑暗的街道亮起點點燈火，一身盛裝的他顯然正要到某處狂歡；當精靈經過時他笑得可大聲呢——雖然他並不知道，此時有位聖誕精靈正和他在一塊呢！

現在，沒有任何預警地，他們又來到一處荒涼、杳無人跡的郊野，奇形怪狀的巨石四散，好像巨人的墳場一樣。水流遍地——或者可以說，過去曾經如此，現在因為寒霜使水面都結冰了——地面上只看得到苔蘚、金雀花及雜草。西方天空中夕陽火紅的餘暉像隻慍怒的眼睛，瞪視著這片荒野，不久那深蹙的眉頭就越來越低，越來越低，終於在濃濃的夜色中消失。

「這是哪裡？」史顧己問。

「礦工居住的地區，他們在地下工作，」精靈回答：「不過，他們認識我。瞧！」

有一間小屋的窗口散發出光芒，他們快速地走向它。穿過一面泥巴牆後，他們發現有一群人愉悅地圍坐在燃燒的火堆旁。一對很老很老的夫妻與他們的孩子，孩子的孩子，甚至是更年輕的一代，都穿上過節的服裝，打扮得十分華麗。老先生正在為大家唱聖誕歌曲，聲音不斷被荒野上呼嘯的風聲蓋過，那是他小時候學會的一首老歌，其他人也不斷地跟著合唱。當然，他們開口時，老先生就更高興，唱得也更大聲了，而他們閉口時，老先生的聲音就再度低沉下來。

精靈並沒有在此久留，他命令史顧己捉住袍子，飛過了荒野。他們急忙前往何處呢？不是去海裡吧？就是到海裡去。史顧己恐懼地往回望，看到土地以及那一大片的岩石都已被遠遠拋在身後。他的耳朵只聽見隆隆的水聲，海浪正洶湧、咆哮、發怒地打在可怕的巨穴之間，並企圖要侵蝕地球。

　　離海岸不遠處，有一塊沒入海中的岩石形成了黝黑的暗礁，終年被海水沖濺侵蝕，上面聳立著一座孤零零的燈塔。一大片的海草盤繞在燈塔的基石上，海鳥——牠們與海草一樣是隨風而生的——在海上起起落落，就像牠們掠過的浪潮一樣。

　　即便是在這裡，兩個守燈的人也生起火——火光從厚重石牆的縫隙中流洩而出，照在可怕駭人的海面上。他們兩人圍坐在一張簡陋的桌子旁，握著彼此長滿厚繭的手，以一壺烈酒互道聖誕快樂。其中較年長的那位，臉上滿是風霜的痕跡，猶如一艘老船的船首雕像，他唱起了聖誕頌歌，歌聲氣勢磅礴，有如外面的暴風一般。

　　精靈再次加速飛過浪濤翻騰的黝黑大海，飛啊，飛啊，直到了離海岸很遠——他是這麼告訴史顧己的——才降落在一艘船上。他們先後站在掌舵的舵手、船首的瞭望員及值哨的軍官身旁；這些人拖長著幽暗鬼魅般的身影站在值班的角落，但每個人都帶著歸航的希望，低哼聖誕歌曲，或懷想著聖誕節，或低聲地向同伴提及過往的聖誕回憶。甲板上的每個人，無論是清醒或睡著了，無論性格是好或壞，在這一天，都會說些好話，分享著聖誕的歡樂氣氛，還會憶起遠方的親人，並且知道他們也正惦念著自己。

　　史顧己感到十分驚訝，當他聽到海風呼嘯，想到在這孤寂黝黑的茫茫大海上，航行是件多麼沉重的事，何況這神秘的大海就如死亡一樣深不可測時，竟然聽到一陣開懷的笑聲。更讓史顧己詫異的是，那竟是他外甥的笑聲，他猛然發現自己正站在一個明亮乾燥的房間，精靈微笑地站在一旁，帶著欣賞與和藹的神色看著外甥。

「哈哈！」史顧己的外甥大笑著，「哈哈哈！」

如果你碰巧認識一個笑聲比史顧己的外甥更痛快的人——其實不太可能——我只能說，我想認識他。請把他介紹給我，我會與他成為好友的。

世事總是如此公平——疾病及憂愁會傳染，但是沒有任何事物比笑聲及幽默更具感染力。當史顧己的外甥捧著肚皮，晃著腦袋瓜，笑得連臉都誇張地扭曲時，他的妻子也在旁邊開懷大笑。他們一旁的朋友也不落人後，笑聲更是響徹雲霄呢。

「哈哈！哈哈哈哈！」

「我說真的，他說耶誕節根本就是亂來！」史顧己的外甥尖叫著說，「他是真的這樣想的。」

「弗瑞德，這真是可恥啊！」史顧己的外甥媳氣憤地叫道。上帝保佑這些女人，她們做事從來不會半調子，總是非常認真。

她很美，美麗絕倫。姣好的臉蛋上有兩個迷人的酒窩，及令人想一親芳澤的櫻桃小嘴——無疑地，一定有人這麼做了；下巴上則有許多小痣，當她笑起來時，都融化在一起了；而那對閃閃動人的雙眸，絕對是你見過最迷人的眼睛。

總而言之，你知道的，她就是人們所謂的迷人女孩，但也讓人看了很舒服。噢，非常地舒服。

「他是個滑稽的老頭，」史顧己的外甥說道，「真的，而且也不是很討人喜歡。不過，他這樣無禮，自然會有報應，我無須再多說什麼了。」

「弗瑞德，我敢說他一定很有錢，」史顧己的外甥媳說：「至少，你總是這樣跟我說的。」

「那又怎樣呢？親愛的。」史顧己的外甥回答，「他的財富對他一點用處都沒有。他不會好好利用它，也沒有因此過得更舒服。甚至，只要一想到這筆財產將來要留給我們，他就渾身不舒服——哈哈哈！」

「我真受不了他。」史顧己的外甥媳發表自己的意見，她的姊妹以及其他女士也都表示同樣的看法。

「噢，還好啦！」史顧己的外甥說道：「我覺得他有點可憐，不過就是無法對他生氣。他有那些不好的念頭，受害的又會是誰呢？其實就是他自己。他不喜歡我們，所以不來跟我們一起用餐。結果呢？說真的，他確實也沒有錯過什麼豐盛的晚餐。」

「事實上，我想他錯過了一頓非常棒的晚餐。」史顧己的外甥媳插嘴道。其他每個人也都這麼認為，他們也都有資格這麼說，因為他們才剛用過晚餐，甜點還擺在桌上，大家都圍聚在火爐邊。

「噢！我很高興聽到妳這麼說，」史顧己的外甥說道，

「因為我對現在這些年輕的主婦沒多大信心。塔普，你認為呢？」

塔普顯然看上了史顧己外甥媳的妹妹，因為他回答說，他沒資格發表意見，像他這樣的單身漢就猶如可憐的流浪漢，無權發表意見。這話一說完，史顧己外甥媳的妹妹——戴著蕾絲領巾，身段豐腴的那位，不是繫著玫瑰的那一個——因此紅了臉。

「弗瑞德，繼續說下去，」史顧己的外甥媳拍著手說道：「這個人總是話說到一半！真是無可救藥！」

史顧己的外甥又開始大笑，他的笑聲無可避免地感染眾人，儘管那豐腴的妹妹努力地想以嗅聞芳香醋來避免發笑，但大家都還是隨著史顧己的外甥大笑起來。

「我只是想說，」史顧己的外甥說道，「我覺得，他討厭我們、不跟我們一起過節的結果就是，他錯過了一些愉快時光，而這些時刻對他一點壞處也沒有。我很確定，在他的腦海中，或是在那間陳腐老舊的辦公室，還是他骯髒的屋子裡，都找不到這樣討喜的夥伴。無論他喜不喜歡，我每年都企圖給他一次機會，因為我同情他。他可以一直嘲諷聖誕節到他死掉為止，但我要向他挑戰。假如他發現我年復一年都到他那裡，好聲好氣地對他說：『史顧己舅舅，你好嗎？』一定能讓他對聖誕節改觀。假如這能夠讓他心血來潮留下五十英鎊給他可憐的職員，那也算是有點意義囉。而且，我覺得昨天他被我打動了。」

第二個精靈

　　當他提到他打動了史顧己，其他人又笑了起來。不過，史顧己的外甥脾氣非常好，也不在乎其他人到底在笑什麼，他繼續鼓動大家歡樂的情緒，快快樂樂地傳著酒瓶。

　　喝過酒後，他們開始唱歌。因為他們都很喜愛音樂，所以，我可以向你保證，不論是合唱或輪唱都是有模有樣。尤其是塔普，就像個絕佳的男低音，絕不會有頭冒青筋，或臉紅脖子粗的情形。史顧己的外甥媳彈得一手好豎琴，她彈了幾首曲子，其中夾雜著一首簡單的小曲（真的挺簡單，你大概聽個兩分鐘就可以跟著哼了），正是當年從寄宿學校把史顧己帶回家的小女孩所熟悉的歌曲，過去的聖誕精靈曾經喚醒史顧己這段回憶；當這首歌曲的旋律出現，精靈呈現給他看過的影像又一一浮現腦海。史顧己越來越軟化，他心想，若幾年前就能夠經常聽到這首曲子，那他應該能以自己的雙手創造出屬於自己的幸福，而無須依賴教堂執事那把埋葬了雅各・馬利的鐵鏟了。

　　他們並不是整個晚上都在唱歌。過了一會兒，他們開始玩起處罰遊戲，偶爾能當當小孩也不錯，何況是在耶誕時分，因為，耶誕節紀念的不就是個剛誕生的嬰孩嗎？慢著！他們還先玩了捉迷藏呢──這是一定要的囉！而我實在不相信塔普真的看不見，我想他的眼睛一定長在靴子上了。我覺得，他和史顧己的外甥已經串通好了，而現在的耶誕精靈也知道。塔普追在戴著蕾絲領巾的胖妹妹身後的模樣，對輕信人性的人來說是一種侮辱。他一會兒撞到火爐，一會兒跌落在椅上，一會兒又碰到鋼琴，一會兒又差點把自己悶死在窗簾裡，但無論胖妹妹跑到哪，他就是可以找到哪。他總是知道她身在何方，絕不會捉到其他的人。如果你像他們一些人一樣，碰巧跑到他面前，他會佯裝出要捉你的模樣——這對你的智商實在是一種侮辱——然後很快地又轉身去追那個胖妹妹了。那個胖妹妹嘴裡一直嚷著這不公平，的確是很不公平沒錯。最後，他終於捉到她了——儘管她快速地在他身邊跑來跑去，蕾絲衣物不斷地沙沙作響，他還是將她逼到角落，讓她無法脫逃。他接下來的行為更惡劣了——他假裝不知道捉到的人是誰，趁機摸摸她的頭飾，並佯裝要確認對方的身分，進一步觸碰她手上的戒指及脖子上的項鍊——這真是卑鄙下流的行為！後來換了另一個人當鬼，這兩人一起偷躲在窗簾後面時，她想必一定會藉此對他表示自己的感受吧。

史顧己的外甥媳並沒有加入捉迷藏遊戲，而是舒舒服服地坐在大椅子上，雙腳擱在一張腳凳上，此時史顧己與精靈就在離她不遠處。不過她後來就加入了處罰遊戲，並且用盡所有的字母來表達對遊戲中愛人的情意。接下來的問答遊戲中，她的表現更是棒極了，而讓史顧己的外甥暗地感到高興的是，她擊敗了她的姊妹們；不過，或許塔普已經告訴過你，那些女孩可也是很厲害的呢。這裡老老少少共約有二十來人，全部都加入遊戲，史顧己亦是其中之一。因為他對眼前的一切太過熱衷，以致於忘記他們根本聽不到他的聲音，

不時情不自禁地大聲說出自己的答案，還經常都猜對了呢。即使是「白教堂牌」那保證不會在針眼處斷裂的上等縫針，也不比史顧己敏銳，儘管他希望自己遲鈍一點。

精靈很高興看到史顧己這麼開心，尤其當史顧己像個孩子般地要求多待一會兒時，精靈更流露出關切的眼神，但他說這是沒辦法的事。

「又有新遊戲了，」史顧己說道，「再半個鐘頭，精靈，半個鐘頭就好！」

這個新遊戲叫做「是或否」，史顧己的外甥必須先在腦中想一件東西，讓其他人來猜；他們可以提出問題，但史顧己的外甥只能針對問題回答是或不是。在猛烈的質問炮火攻擊下，史顧己的外甥說他想的是一種動物，活生生的動物，而且很難相處，又殘忍，有時會發出咆哮咕噥的聲音，有時會說話，住在倫敦，會沿著街道走路，但不是讓人觀看或由任何人飼養的動物，也不是住在動物園，市場攤販也不曾宰殺過，不是馬、驢、乳牛、公牛、老虎、狗或豬，也不是貓或熊。每當有人提出問題，史顧己的外甥就會迸出大笑，有時甚至笑到不得不自沙發起身跺腳。最後，那個胖妹妹跟史顧己一樣開始大笑，高聲叫道：「我知道答案了！弗瑞德，我知道那是什麼了！我知道了！」

「是什麼？」弗瑞德喊道。

「是你的舅舅──史、顧、己！」

答案的確是史顧己。這答案獲得了一致的讚賞，儘管有人提出異議，認為當他們問「是頭熊嗎」，史顧己的外甥並沒有回答「是」，這否定的答案誤導了他們，使得他們把史顧己先生剔出名單外，一副他們曾經把他列入名單中考慮的模樣。

「老實說，他已經為我們帶來許多歡樂啦！」弗瑞德說道：「如果我們不為他的健康乾一杯的話，就實在是太不知感恩了。現在，大家手邊都有一杯溫酒，讓我說：『敬史顧己舅舅！』」

「好吧！敬史顧己舅舅！」他們一起大喊。

「無論他現在身處何方，都要祝這位老人聖誕快樂及新年快樂！」史顧己的外甥說道，「他不接受我的祝福，但我仍要祝他快樂，敬史顧己舅舅！」

史顧己舅舅的心頭慢慢地感到輕鬆愉快，假如精靈再多給他一點時間，他也會回敬這群沒有察覺他存在的人，並以他們聽不見的長篇大論來表達謝意。但在史顧己的外甥吐出最後一個字的瞬間，全部的景象就消失了。史顧己與精靈又踏上旅途。

他們看了好多東西，走了很多路，拜訪了很多家庭，大多數的家庭都擁有快樂的夜晚。精靈來到病床邊，病人就開心起來；精靈站到遊子身邊，遊子就有歸鄉的感覺；它來到努力掙扎的人身旁，這些人就對自己的夢想多了一份執著；站在貧窮人的身旁，他們就感到心頭富裕。在救濟院、醫院、監獄、每個苦難庇護所裡，只要自負的守門人沒有利用他短暫的小小職權將大門鎖上，使得精靈被擋在門外，它就會留下祝福，並以此告誡史顧己。

如果這只是一個晚上的時間，還真是個漫長的夜晚啊；但史顧己卻對此感到好奇，因為整個耶誕假期似乎都凝縮在他們共同相處的這個晚上。更奇怪的是，史顧己的外貌並沒有任何改變，但精靈則明顯地變老了。史顧己注意到這種改變，不過卻沒有說出。直到他們離開了某個孩童的「十二夜節」派對，來到一個空曠的地方後，史顧己發現精靈的頭髮已然灰白。

「精靈的生命都很短暫嗎？」史顧己問道。

「我在這個星球上的生命相當短暫，」精靈回答，「今晚我的生命就結束了。」

「今晚！」史顧己驚叫。

「今天午夜。聽！時間快到了。」

此時，十一點三刻的鐘聲響起。

「恕我冒昧，」史顧己專注地看著精靈的長袍，「但是我發現，你的袍子下面有奇怪的東西伸出來，那應該不是你的身體。那是腳還是爪子呢？」

「從上面的皮膚看來，那或許是爪子。」精靈哀傷地回答，「你看這裡。」

精靈從袍子摺疊之處領出兩個小孩，他們衣著破爛，全身髒兮兮的，面容醜惡，令人害怕。他們跪倒在精靈的腳邊，並緊緊捉住長袍。

第二個精靈

「喂!看這裡,看,快看,在下面這裡。」精靈尖叫道。

這兩個小孩,一男一女,面黃肌瘦,衣裳襤褸,滿面愁容且帶著敵意,卻也因為卑微而面帶沮喪。孩童臉上原本該有的年輕氣息及青春的色彩,現在卻恍若被一隻枯槁的手——就如歲月之手——蹂躪、摧殘得不成人形。他們應該像天使般純潔的,現在卻充滿惡意,有如妖魔纏身。無論偉大的造物者用何種奇妙的方法讓人性改變、墮落、退化,都不會有這怪物一半的恐怖駭人。

史顧已大吃一驚,嚇得往後退。看到眼前這幅景象,就算他想說他們是好孩子,也無法道出這麼一個漫天大謊。

「精靈,這是你的孩子嗎?」史顧已只能這麼說。

「是人類的孩子。」精靈看著孩子說道,「他們從祖先身旁逃走,緊跟著我。男的叫『無知』,女的則叫『貧困』。要提防他們以及他們的同類,尤其要注意這個男孩,因為我看到他的眉宇之間寫著『宿命』,除非能將它抹去,否則宿命無可避免。」精靈伸直手臂指向城市大喊:「你們儘管否認吧!儘管去中傷那些說出事實的人吧!儘管為了爭權奪利而容許這些事實存在,然後讓情況變得更糟!你們會得到報應的!」

「他們沒有任何避難之處或資源吧?」史顧已大聲問道。

「難道沒有監獄嗎?」精靈最後一次模仿他的話,「難道沒有聯合貧民習藝所嗎？」

十二點的鐘聲響了。

史顧己看看四周，精靈不見了。最後一道鐘聲漸漸平息後，史顧己想起老雅各‧馬利的預言。他抬起眼便看到一位身披長袍、圍著頭巾、神情嚴肅的精靈，猶如一陣飄過地面的霧似地朝他而來。

第四樂章

最後一個精靈

　　精靈緩慢且嚴肅地悄悄靠近。當它接近時，史顧己不禁跪倒在地上，因為精靈所遊走的空氣中，散發著一股極為幽暗神秘的氣息。

　　精靈全身上下覆蓋著一件黑色的長袍，使得它的頭、臉、身體都無法辨識，除了一隻伸出來的手。要不是那隻手，實在很難在黑夜中分辨出它的形體。

　　精靈來到史顧己的身邊時，他覺得它既高大又威嚴，而且它那神秘的氣質使他敬畏。他所知道的就這麼多了，因為精靈一言不發，也沒有任何動作。

　　「在我面前的是未來的聖誕精靈吧？」史顧己問。

　　精靈沒有回答，只是用手指著前方。

　　「你要讓我看的幻影是現在未發生、但將來一定會發生的景象嗎？」史顧己繼續追問，「精靈，是這樣嗎？」

　　精靈長袍上半部的皺褶瞬間縮動了一下，彷彿精靈正面點了一下頭──這也是史顧己唯一得到的答案。

　　儘管史顧己此時已經很習慣精靈的陪伴，但他對眼前這沉默的形體仍感到非常害怕；他的雙腿抖得厲害，甚至當他準備隨著精靈去時，居然連站都站不好。精靈注意到他的情況，便停頓片刻，讓他恢復鎮定。

不過史顧己的情況卻變得更糟。一種模糊、不明確的恐懼感使他不停地發抖，他知道在那團黝黑的長袍後面，精靈鬼魅般的雙眼正定定地注視著他；儘管他已盡可能地伸直身子，但除了精靈的手以及一團黑外，他根本看不到任何東西。

「未來的精靈啊！」史顧己叫道，「你是我見過最令人畏懼的精靈。但我知道你的目的是為了我好。我希望以後能脫胎換骨，也已準備心存感激地接受你的陪伴。你難道不開口跟我說話嗎？」

精靈沒有回應，手直直地指向前方。

「帶路吧！」史顧己說，「帶路吧！夜晚過得如此地快。我知道，時間對我來說異常寶貴。所以，精靈，帶路吧！」

精靈開始飄移——一如之前它來到史顧己面前的方式。史顧己尾隨著精靈長袍的影子，覺得那個黑影讓他浮了起來，帶著他走。

與其說他們進入了城鎮，不如說是城鎮在他們周遭冒了出來，並且將他們團團包圍。總之他們來到了市中心，站在交易所裡，旁邊盡是一群生意人——有的人匆匆忙忙地跑來跑去，有的人把玩著口袋裡的錢幣，有的人圍繞在一起交談，有的人低頭看錶，有的人則一面撥弄著大大的金印章一面細細思考……史顧己對這些景象非常熟悉。

精靈在一小群生意人旁邊停下了腳步。史顧已看到精靈用手指著他們，便向前傾聽他們說話。

　　「不，」一個有著雙下巴的胖男人說道，「我也知道得不多，我只知道他死了。」

　　「他什麼時候死的呢？」另一個人詢問。

　　「我想，是昨晚吧。」

　　「天啊，他怎麼啦？」第三個人拿出一個很大的鼻菸盒，吸了一大口鼻菸：「我還以為他永遠不會死咧。」

　　「天知道。」胖男人打了個呵欠回答道。

　　「他的財產怎麼處理呢？」一個臉龐紅通通的男人問道，他鼻頭上一個肉瘜晃啊晃的，看來就像火雞頸下的肉瘤。

　　「這倒還沒聽說，」雙下巴的男人回答，又打了一次呵欠：「或許會留給他的公司吧。我能確定的是：他不會把錢留給我。」

　　這句玩笑話引來哄堂大笑。

　　「他的葬禮一定很簡陋，」那個胖男人又說，「因為我還沒聽說有誰打算參加的。我們組個自願團，如何？」

　　「如果有提供午餐的話，我倒不介意去參加。」鼻頭長有肉瘜的男人說，「但是要我去，就要有得吃。」

　　又是另一陣笑聲。

　　「那麼，我可能是對此事最不感興趣的人了，」胖男人說道，「因為我從未戴過黑手套，也從未吃過這種午餐。不過要是其他人要去的話，我還是樂意前往。想一想，我大概是他最特別的朋友了，因為我們碰面時，可經常會停下來說話呢。各位再見了！」

這群人散了開來，各自加入其他小圈子的談話。史顧己認識這些人，他看著精靈，希望得到解釋。

精靈又飄到街上，手指向兩個正在講話的人。史顧己只好再次傾聽這兩人的談話內容，心想或許可以從這邊得到答案。

他跟這兩個人也很熟。他們兩個也是商人，非常富有，地位舉足輕重。史顧己時常希望自己的意見能獲得他們的尊敬——當然，只限於商場上的意見。

「你好。」其中一個人打了聲招呼。

「你好。」另一個人也回應。

「對了，」第一個人說道：「惡魔終於帶走他了，是嗎？」

「我也聽說了。」第二個人回答，「好冷喔，不是嗎？」

「耶誕節一向如此。我想，你不溜冰嗎？」

「不，不。還有別的事要忙。再見了！」

他們的對話只有這樣。他們就這樣碰面，短短地交談幾句，然後就又分道揚鑣了。

史顧己先是有點驚訝，精靈竟然會認為這瑣碎的對話很重要，但他又隱約覺得，這背後一定有什麼深意。他開始猜

想，他們指的應該不是馬利過世這件事，因為那是過去式了，而這個精靈所掌管的是未來。但他實在想不出來，到底是哪個與自己有關的人可以跟這番話搭得上勾。不過，可以確定的是，無論他們指的是誰，這一定對他的自我改善有所幫助。他決定要好好記住每個聽到的字眼，以及看到的每件事情。尤其，若他未來的身影出現時，更是要注意，因為他期待未來的他能夠提供一些遺漏的訊息，讓他可以輕易地解開這謎團。

他四處找尋未來的自己，不過他只看見另一個人站在他熟悉的角落裡。儘管時間已指向他平常會出現的時刻，但從交易所玄關湧入的眾多人潮中，他卻看不到自己的身影。不過，他倒也不怎麼詫異，因為他已經決定要脫胎換骨，也希望可以看到自己新生的模樣。

站在他身旁的精靈靜默且陰沉，只伸出一隻手。當史顧己從沉思中回過神來，他突然從那隻手的方向，以及精靈與自身的位置中，明白精靈那雙神秘的眼睛正盯著他。他不禁渾身發冷，不停地發抖。

他們離開這繁忙的景象，來到城鎮裡較為晦暗的地區。史顧己從未到過這裡，不過他一眼就認出這個惡名昭彰的地方。這裡的街道非常骯髒狹窄，一旁的鋪子及住家看起來都破破爛爛的；居民個個衣衫不整，面貌醜陋，醉醺醺的，一副懶洋洋的模樣；巷弄及拱廊就跟汙水溝一樣骯髒，將惡臭、垃圾及人都嘔到髒亂的街道上 —— 整個地區瀰漫著罪惡、汙穢及悲慘的氣息。

在這個聲名狼藉的深處，有一間屋簷低矮、店面突出的鋪子，專門收購廢鐵、舊布、瓶罐、骨頭及油膩膩的廢棄物等；鋪子樓上則堆滿了生鏽的鑰匙、鐵釘、鏈子、絞鏈、銼刀、台秤、砝碼及各種破銅爛鐵。

幾乎沒人想探究的秘密，就隱藏在這堆積如山的破布、腐敗的油脂團及骨頭堆積出來的墓穴中。在這堆貨品當中，有一個年逾七十歲、頭髮已經灰白的老頭子，正坐在用老磚砌成的木炭爐子旁。這個老頭以繩子掛上各種破布縫製成的臭窗簾，用以阻擋外頭的冷空氣，然後平靜地享受吞雲吐霧之樂。

史顧已與精靈來到這裡時，正巧有個婦人背了一袋重重的東西悄悄進入店裡。她剛進來沒多久，另一個婦人也背著一大捆東西進來了，後面緊跟著又進來一個穿著褪色黑衣的男人。男人看到這兩個女人時嚇了一跳，而當他們認出彼此時，更是吃了一驚。他們吃驚得說不出話來，抽著菸的老頭也愣住了，他們三個人這才爆出笑聲。

「清潔婦最先來到！」第一個進來的女人叫道：「第二個是洗衣婦，最後是葬儀社的人！看，老喬，這真巧哪！我們可沒約好呢。」

「這裡可是你們碰面的最佳場所，」老喬拿下嘴邊的菸說道，「進廳裡來吧。妳啊，老早以前就在這大廳自由自在地進進出出了，其他兩個人也不是新客。等等，讓我先鎖上

門。噢，好刺耳啊！我想，沒有哪塊廢金屬比這絞鏈生鏽得
還厲害了，大概也沒有哪根老骨頭比我還老囉。哈，哈！我
們跟自己的職業都配得很呢，非常適合。進大廳，進大廳
吧。」

大廳在破布窗簾後面。老頭子用一根老舊的階梯棒將火
撥弄在一塊兒，然後用菸管清了清冒煙的燈芯（因為已經天
黑了），才又再度將菸放入口中。

他在做這些動作的同時，剛剛開口講話的清潔婦則把自
己那一大袋東西丟到地板上，隨後便大搖大擺地在凳子上坐
下；她手肘交疊放在膝蓋上，帶著敵意看向另外兩個人。

「那又怎樣呢！狄柏太太，那又怎樣呢？」女人說道，
「誰不為自己打算？『他』向來如此。」

「的確沒錯！」洗衣婦說，「沒人比得上他。」

「所以呢，妳就別站在那邊乾瞪眼，一副害怕的模樣。
這裡都是聰明人吧？我想，我們不會互揭瘡疤吧。」

「當然不會！」狄柏太太和另一個男人異口同聲地回
答，「我們不希望如此。」

「那就好啦！」女人叫道，「這就夠了。丟幾樣東西，
會對誰造成損失呢？我想，答案絕不會是已經死掉的人
吧。」

「那當然囉。」狄柏太太笑著說。

「假如這個邪惡的老守財奴死後還想保有這些東西，」
女人繼續說，「他活著時幹嘛不結婚生子？這樣，他在與死

神搏鬥時，才會有人照料他，而不至於孤零零地嚥下最後一口氣。」

「這些話說得再真確不過了，」狄柏太太說道，「這是他的報應。」

「我希望報應再重一點，」女人回答，「而且本來就該如此。假如我可以再多拿走一些東西就好了。老喬，打開那個包袱，幫我估個價，你就坦白說吧。我不怕當第一個，也不怕他們看到。我們都很清楚，在我們碰面之前所做的，不過是自我救濟。我想，這不是什麼罪過。老喬，打開包袱吧。」

不過他的兩個朋友可不允許她這麼做。穿著褪色黑衣的男人率先取出他的戰利品，東西並不多，只有兩個印章、一個鉛筆盒、一對袖釦及一只便宜的胸針。老喬逐一拿起來檢視、估價，並用粉筆在牆上寫下每樣物品的價格，最後才加總起來。

「這是你應得的數目。」老喬說，「即使殺了我，我也不願再多出一毛錢。下一個？」

輪到狄柏太太。她拿出幾條床單與毛巾、幾件衣服、兩支老式的銀湯匙，一對糖夾，以及幾雙靴子。每樣東西的價格也都記錄在牆上。

「我對女人總是大方一點，這是我的毛病，也是讓我毀了自己的原因。」老喬說，「這是妳應得的價錢。如果妳要跟我多討一塊錢，我可要反悔自己太大方，還要再多扣妳半克朗。」

　　「喬，現在換我了。」清潔婦說道。

　　喬跪了下來，好打開包袱。他鬆了好幾個結，然後拉出一捲又大又重的黑色東西。

　　「這叫什麼來著？」老喬說，「床帷！」

　　「噢！」女人回答，邊笑邊抱著手臂往前傾，「床帷！」

　　「妳不會告訴我，他還沒嚥氣，妳就把床帷、環釦什麼的拆下來吧？」老喬問。

　　「沒錯，」女人回答，「有何不可呢？」

　　「妳有發財命，」老喬說，「妳的確會發財。」

　　「像他這種人，我絕不會手下留情的。喬，我敢這樣跟你說，只要我摸得到的東西，我都不放過。」女人冷酷地答道，「現在，小心點，別讓油滴到羊毛毯了。」

　　「他的羊毛毯？」喬發問。

　　「要不然你認為會是誰的？」女人回答，「我敢說呀，就算沒有毯子，他也不會覺得冷啊。」

　　「我希望他不是因為什麼傳染病死的，不是吧？」老喬停下動作，抬起眼看她。

　　「你別怕，」清潔婦回答，「假如是這樣的話，像我這麼討厭他的人才不會在他旁邊晃那麼久。噢！你大可以檢查那件襯衫，保證你找到眼睛發疼也絕對找不到任何破洞或露線的地方。那是他最好的一件襯衫，也真是件高級貨。如果

我沒拿走的話，那可就浪費了。」

「你說浪費是什麼意思？」老喬問。

「當然啊，他們會讓他穿著這件襯衫入土，」女人笑著回答：「竟然有人會笨得如此做，幸好我又把它脫下來了。假如此時不穿白棉布襯衫，那該什麼時候穿啊？他穿白棉布襯衫倒挺合身的，也不會醜到哪裡去。」

史顧己心驚膽跳地聽著這段對話。當他看到那群人在老頭子的微弱燈光下，圍著戰利品討論時，他感到深惡痛絕。就算眼前是一群面目可憎的惡魔正在商討販售屍體的事宜，都還不至於讓史顧己如此深惡痛絕。

老喬此時把裝滿錢幣的法蘭絨袋取出，開始一一算起地上戰利品的價格，清潔婦則笑道：「哈哈！你看，下場就是這樣！他活著時把每一個人都嚇跑了，結果他死後反而讓我們得利。哈哈哈！」

「精靈！」史顧己全身上下都在顫抖，「我懂了，我懂了。這個死去的人可能就是我。照我目前的情況，我的下場可能就是如此。慈悲的上帝啊，這是什麼下場！」

場景再度改變了。他的手幾乎碰觸到床鋪，但他卻因害怕而退卻。那是一張空無一物，連床帷都沒有的床鋪，上面只有一條破床巾，底下似乎蓋著什麼東西，儘管沒有任何動靜，但卻以恐怖的語言宣示自身的存在。

房間很暗，以致於無法清楚辨識一切，儘管如此，史顧己仍好奇地張望周遭，急切地想知道這是什麼房間。一道微弱的光線從外面直射在床鋪上，躺在上頭的，正是那個被剝奪一空，沒有人看顧、照料或為他哭泣的男人屍體。

史顧己瞄了精靈一眼。精靈的手定定地指著屍體的頭部。床巾隨隨便便地蓋著，只要史顧己用手指稍微往上掀，屍體的臉就會整個顯露出來。史顧己心想，這動作易如反掌，自己也非常渴望這麼做，卻沒有力量去掀開那張床單，就像他無力趕走身旁的精靈一樣。

噢，冷酷、莊嚴且可怕的死亡之神，祢在這裡擺下了祭壇，並且以祢所能支配的恐怖來裝飾吧，這可是由祢主宰啊！但對於一個受人喜愛、尊敬及崇仰的人，祢就無法動他們一根寒毛，或者讓他們變得面目可憎。這並不是因為他們解脫時，雙手沉重且垂落，也不是因為他們的心臟或脈搏仍在跳動，而是因為他們的雙手曾是慷慨好施且真誠，他們的心曾經勇敢、溫暖且溫柔，他們的脈搏也曾流動著人類的熱血。攻擊吧，精靈，攻擊吧！看看他傷口所湧出的善行，那會使得這個世界的生命永生不息。

並沒有人在史顧己耳邊說這些話，但他看著床鋪時，耳邊卻響起這些話。史顧己心想，若這個人現在能死而復生，第一個產生的念頭不知是什麼？欲望、競爭激烈的生意，還是緊握利益不放？這些念頭讓他走得多風光啊！

在這空蕩蕩的漆黑屋子裡，只有他一個人躺在那裡，沒有任何大人或小孩陪伴在他身邊，述說他曾對他們多麼和善，或說因為他曾講過的一句好話，所以他們必須陪著他。

一隻貓正抓著門板，而爐邊則有老鼠嚙咬東西的聲音。在這個躺了死人的房間裡，牠們接下來想要做什麼呢？他們又為何如此騷動？史顧己不敢多想。

「精靈！」史顧己說，「這個地方太恐怖了。相信我，我絕不會忘記這個教訓。我們離開好嗎？我們走吧！」

精靈仍動也不動地指著床鋪。

「我知道你的意思，」史顧己回答，「如果我做得到，我一定會照做。可是我無能為力呀，精靈，我真的沒有那個勇氣。」

精靈再次看著他。

「假如這個城鎮有人因為這個男人的死亡而悲傷，」史顧己相當苦悶地說道，「請帶我去看看吧。我求求你，精靈！」

瞬間，精靈在他前方猶如展翅一般地揮開長袍，然後又收了回去。眼前出現的是一間有著日光照耀的屋子，裡面有一個母親和她的幾個孩子。

母親正焦慮地等著某人，她在房裡走來走去，一聽到聲音就驚跳起來，並焦急地望向窗外，一會兒又瞄了瞄時鐘，一會兒拿起針線，但又徒勞地放下，她甚至無法忍受孩童玩鬧的聲音。

最後，她期待的敲門聲響起了，她急忙衝到門邊迎接。她的丈夫很年輕，但那張臉卻十分憔悴沮喪。不過，此刻他臉上出現一種奇特的神情，一種令他覺得差恥，極力想壓抑的高興神色。

他在火爐邊坐下來，吃起那些為他準備好的晚餐。他們沉默許久後，她虛弱地開口問他有沒有什麼新消息，他顯然有些尷尬，不知該如何作答。

「好消息？還是壞消息？」她試著幫他開口。

「壞消息。」他回答。

「我們真的破產了？」

「不。卡洛琳，還有一線希望在。」

「假如他大發慈悲，的確是有希望！」她驚訝地說道，「要是真有這樣的奇蹟發生，還有什麼事沒希望呢？」

「他沒有大發慈悲，」她的丈夫說，「但是他死了。」

如果她臉上的表情沒有作假的話，那她顯然是一個溫柔且具包容力的女人；但她聽到這句話，卻打從心裡感激，並雙手合十說出自己的感受。過了片刻，她便感到抱歉，並請求上帝寬恕，然而她的第一個舉動卻將她內心的想法表露無遺。

「當我想試著見他，求他讓我們延緩一個禮拜再清還債款時，昨晚我跟妳提過的那個半醉半清醒的女人告訴我這個消息。我本來以為這只是一個避開我的藉口，但消息是真的。那個時候，他不只病得很嚴重，而且就快死了。」

「那我們的債務要還給誰呢？」

「我不知道，但在那之前，我們就能將錢準備好了。就算沒有準備好，要碰到像他那麼殘酷的債主，運氣也真是太差了。總之，我們今晚可以安心睡覺了，卡洛琳！」

是的，他們的確寬心不少。圍繞在他們四周沉默傾聽的孩子，儘管不太懂他們的談話內容，臉蛋也亮了起來。這個男人的死竟然為這個家帶來歡樂！精靈給他看因這個事件所引發的一切情緒，竟然只有歡樂。

「讓我看看因為這件事而難過的人，」史顧己說，「要不然我們剛離開的那間暗房間，將會永遠烙印在我的腦海啊。」

精靈帶著史顧己穿過幾條他熟悉的街道。當他們前進時，史顧己不停地四處張望，想找尋自己的身影，卻一無所獲。他們來到之前史顧己拜訪過的地方──可憐的鮑勃克勞契的家。屋子裡，母親與孩子們正圍坐在火爐旁。

一片靜默。非常地安靜。幾個吵鬧的小孩現在都安靜得像尊雕像，乖乖地坐在角落，望著正在看書的長子彼得。母親與女兒正忙著做針線活，她們也非常地安靜。

「耶穌叫了個孩子過來，讓他站在他們之間。」

史顧己在哪裡聽過這些話？他不是在作夢。一定是在精靈與史顧己跨過門廊時，那個男孩大聲唸出來的。他怎麼不繼續唸下去呢？

母親將針線活放在桌上，雙手摀住臉。

「那個顏色太刺眼了。」她解釋道。

顏色？噢，可憐的小提姆！

「現在又好一點了，」克勞契太太說道，「在燭光下做活的話眼睛很吃力，你們父親回家時，我可不要讓他看到我疲憊的雙眼。是他到家的時間了。」

「已經超過時間，」彼得闔上書，回答道，「我想他走的速度大概比平常慢了一點，這幾天總是這樣，媽媽。」

他們又再度沉默。最後，她終於強顏歡笑——中間只結巴了一次——說道，「我知道他以前……我知道他以前扛著小提姆，走得很快呢。」

「我也知道，」彼得大聲說道，「向來如此。」

「我也知道！」另一個人叫道，接著所有人都嚷了起來。

「不過小提姆很輕，」母親重新專注在針線活上，「而且他的父親這麼疼愛他，所以一點都不麻煩……不麻煩。你們父親回來了。」

她急急跑上前去迎接他，而戴著圍巾的小鮑勃——可憐的男人——走了進來。他的茶已擱在壁爐旁的鍋架上，大家都爭先恐後地要幫他端來。接著，兩個年幼的小孩爬上鮑勃的膝蓋，分別將小小的臉頰貼上他的臉，彷彿正在訴說：「爸爸，不要擔心，不要悲傷。」

和自己的家人待在一塊兒，鮑勃感到非常開心，他高興地跟大家談話。他看著桌子上的針線活，讚美起克勞契太太與女兒們的勤勞敏捷。他說，禮拜天之前應該就能完成了。

「禮拜天！所以，鮑勃，你今天去了？」他的妻子問道。

「是的，親愛的，」鮑勃回答，「我真希望妳也一起去。看看那是多麼綠意盎然的一個地方，妳應該會好受一點。不過，妳以後去的機會多的是。我跟他保證，我禮拜天會去那裡走走。我的孩子，我的孩子啊！」鮑勃哭泣著說：「我的孩子！」

　　他忽然崩潰了，無法自抑地哭泣。要是他能忍住，他跟他的孩子也不會那麼親近。

　　他離開客廳走到樓上的房間，裡頭的燈光愉快地閃耀，還布置了聖誕禮物。孩子拉來一張椅子，上面還留著剛坐過的痕跡。可憐的鮑勃坐了下來，沉思了一會後便打起精神，親了親孩子小小的臉蛋。他對一切都認命了，於是又快快樂樂地下樓。

　　他們一家人圍坐在火爐邊談天，母親與女兒仍繼續做著手邊的活。鮑勃告訴他們，史顧己的外甥非常仁慈，他只不過與他有一面之緣，而那天在街上相遇，自己只不過看來有點沮喪──「只有一點沮喪，你們知道的。」鮑勃補充道──史顧己的外甥關切地問他，是什麼事情使他苦惱。「你們絕不曾見過講話這麼和善的人，所以我便把一切都告訴他了。他回答我：『克勞契先生，我由衷地為您和您的好太太感到遺憾。』無論如何，我就是想不通，他怎麼會知道的。」

　　「親愛的，知道什麼呢？」

　　「知道妳是個好太太呀。」鮑勃回答。

「這是大家都知道的啊！」彼得說。

「說得好呀，兒子！」鮑勃嚷道，「我希望他們都知道。『我由衷地為您的好妻子感到遺憾。』史顧己的外甥給我他的名片，還說：『如果我能幫上什麼忙的話，這是我的地址，請來找我。』」鮑勃大聲說：「其實，倒不是他能幫我們什麼忙，而是他那親切和善的態度真令人高興。就好像他認識小提姆，所以與我們感同身受。」

「我想他一定是個好人。」克勞契太太說。

「親愛的，」鮑勃回答，「如果妳見過他，跟他說過話，妳會更加確定這一點。說真的，若他能為彼得找一份較好的工作，我一點也不會訝異。」

「彼得，你聽聽。」克勞契太太說。

「那麼，」其中一個女兒叫了起來，「彼得將來就能找個伴侶成家了。」

「管好妳自己的事就好。」彼得笑著反駁。

「這也不是不可能，」鮑勃說道，「總有一天會的。親愛的，雖然那一天還很遙遠。但就算將來我們分開了，我敢說我們沒有一個人會忘記我們可憐的小提姆，或忘了我們的別離，是吧？」

「我們絕不會忘的，父親！」他們異口同聲地說。

「我知道，」鮑勃說，「親愛的，雖然他小小年紀，但我知道當我們想起小提姆是多麼溫柔時就不會輕易起爭執了，否則就等於忘了小提姆。」

「絕對不會的，父親！」大家再度異口同聲地叫道。

「我很高興，」小鮑勃說，「我真的很高興。」

克勞契太太親了親鮑勃，他的女兒及兩個年幼的孩子也上前來親吻他，長子彼得則與他握了握手。小提姆的靈魂啊，你童稚的本質來自於上帝哪！

「精靈，」史顧己說，「我可以察覺你快離開我了。我知道，但我不知道你會怎麼離開。可不可以告訴我，我們剛看到的那個行將就木的人是誰呢？」

一如既往——儘管時間不同，史顧己想道：其實，他們之後所看到的這些景象都是沒有次序的，唯一的共通點就是這些都是未來的事情——未來的耶誕精靈又將他送到生意人聚集的地方，而史顧己仍然沒見著自己。事實上，精靈並沒有稍作停留，只是直直往前走，彷彿目的地有什麼吸引人的事物似的，史顧己只好哀求它停一會兒。「我們現在急急忙忙經過的這條巷子，」史顧己說，「是我辦公室所在的地方，已經有好長一段時間了。我看到辦公室了。讓我看看未來的自己是什麼模樣吧！」

精靈停了下來，手卻指向另一處。

「房子在那邊，」史顧己驚呼，「你幹嘛指別的地方？」那無情的手指所指的方向仍然不變。

史顧己奔向辦公室的窗戶，往裡頭看了看，這仍然是一間辦公室，但卻不再屬於他。家具都換了，而坐在椅子上的人也不是他。精靈仍然跟之前一樣指著某處。

史顧己再次跟著精靈，並好奇自己為什麼不見了，又跑到哪裡去了，直到他們來到一座鐵門前他才停止思考。進門前他稍作停頓，四處張望。

這是一座教堂墓園。這樣說來，剛剛快死掉的那個人就躺在這座墓園的土壤下囉，現在他可以知道他的名字了。這真是一個名副其實的墓園。四周的房子將這個地方團團圍住，遍地雜草，植物增長的是死氣而非生命力，因為有太多的屍體埋葬在地下，土壤肥沃得已達飽和。真是一個名副其實的墓地！

精靈站在墓碑間，指向其中一座。史顧己全身發抖地走過去。精靈還是保持原來那副模樣，可是在那莊嚴的外表下，他彷彿看到了一些新的意義，不禁感到恐懼。

「在我走向你所指的墓碑之前，」史顧己說，「回答我一個問題。這些幻影是一定會發生的，還是可能會發生的？」

精靈仍指著它旁邊的那座墓碑。

「從一個人的所做所為便可以看出他未來的命運，如果他不斷持續同樣的行為，結果是必然的。」史顧己說，「但是如果他改變了行為，結果也會跟著改變。你給我看的這些景象就是要告訴我這一點，對不對？」

精靈依然動也不動。

史顧己全身打顫，悄悄地走到它身邊，然後順著精靈指的方向看去，唸出淒涼墓碑上的名字：埃比尼澤·史顧己。

「我就是那個躺在床上的人嗎？」他跪倒在地叫道。

精靈手指移向他，又指向墓碑。

「不，精靈！不，不，不！」

精靈仍指著墓碑。

「精靈！」史顧己緊緊捉住精靈的長袍哭泣道，「聽我說，我已經不是過去的我了。有了這次的交流，我絕對不再是過去的我了。如果我已經沒有希望了，為什麼你們還要讓我看這些幻影呢？」

這隻手第一次晃動了起來。

「仁慈的精靈，」史顧己撲倒在精靈面前繼續說道，「您也憐憫我，同情我。告訴我，如果我改變自己的生活方式，我就可以改變這些幻影！」

那隻仁慈的手顫抖了。

「我會打從心裡尊敬聖誕，並且一直努力保持這樣的心情。我會活在過去、現在與未來，我會將這三個精靈時時牢記在心，我不會忘了你們帶給我的教訓。噢，告訴我，我可以抹去這石碑上的名字！」

在這痛苦的情緒中，史顧已忍不住捉住了精靈的手。精靈試著掙脫，但史顧已苦苦哀求之際，力氣變得很大，把那隻手抓得更緊。精靈用更大的力量推開了他。

正當史顧已最後一次闔掌請求精靈改變他的命運時，他看到它的頭巾與長袍產生了變化，它們慢慢皺縮起來、攤落地面、逐漸變小，最後變成了一根床柱。

第五樂章

尾聲

　　沒錯，這是他的床柱，這是他的床鋪，也是他的房間。而最令他高興的是，眼前這是屬於他的時間，他有機會彌補過去的一切。

　　「我會活在過去、現在與未來！」史顧己爬下床時不斷重複地說道。

　　「我會將這三個精靈時時牢記在心。噢，雅各·馬利！我要為此感謝上帝，感謝聖誕！老雅各啊，我是跪著說的，我是跪著說的！」

　　他滿腦子都是行善的欲望，因之全身激動發熱，甚至使得他啞掉的聲音都不聽指揮。在他與精靈激烈地爭辯時，他激動地啜泣，現在他的臉上滿是淚水。

　　「床帷沒給拆下來，」史顧己將一條床帷挽進手裡，叫道：「這些床帷並沒有給拆下來，掛鉤跟其他東西都還在。都在這裡，我也還在這裡，幻影的景象是可以消除的。是的，是可以消除的，我知道可以的。」

　　此時，他的手不停地撫摸那些衣物；他將衣服的反面掏出或倒著穿上，或拉扯它們，要不就亂扔，讓這些衣服一起跟他放肆。

「我不知道該怎麼做！」史顧己又哭又笑地叫道，並且利用長襪當海蛇，讓自己扮成拉奧孔。「我輕鬆如羽毛，快樂得宛如天使，愉悅得像個孩子。跟個醉鬼一樣頭暈暈的。祝每個人聖誕快樂！祝全世界新年快樂！哈囉！萬歲！哈囉！」

現在，他又蹦又跳地進了客廳，站在裡頭上氣不接下氣地喘著。

「那是煮粥的鍋子！」史顧己叫道，再次蹦蹦跳跳地靠近火爐。「那扇門！雅各·馬利的鬼魂就是從那裡進來的！現在的聖誕精靈就坐在這個角落！這扇窗，我就是透過它看到遊蕩的精靈！沒錯，這一切都是真實的，一切的確都發生過了！哈哈哈！」

的確，對於一個多年不曾笑過的人來說，這笑聲真是中氣十足，幾乎要響徹雲霄，也開啟了後面一連串長長的燦爛笑聲。

「我不知道今天是幾號！」史顧己說，「我不知道自己跟精靈在一起多久了。我什麼都不知道，像個新生兒。沒關係，我才不在乎。我寧願當個小嬰兒。哈囉！萬歲！哈囉！」

他欣喜若狂的情緒被教堂的鐘聲給打斷了，那是他聽過最響亮的聲音。鏗鏘，叮咚，鐘聲響。鐘聲響，叮咚，鏗鏘！噢，棒極了！棒極了！

他跑到窗邊並打開窗戶探出頭。沒有濃霧，只有晴朗、明亮、歡樂、熱鬧、寒冷。寒冷空氣的刺激，讓人的血液舞動起來。黃橙橙的陽光，迷人的天空，甜美清新的空氣，歡樂的鐘聲。噢，棒極了！棒極了！

「今天是什麼日子？」史顧己朝著下頭一位盛裝的男孩叫道，那男孩可能正在附近閒蕩偷看他。

「啊？」男孩驚訝地出聲。

「好孩子，今天是什麼日子？」史顧己說。

「今天？」男孩回答，「天啊，是聖誕節啊。」

「今天是聖誕節！」史顧己對自己說，「我沒錯過。精靈只用一個晚上就給我看了那麼多影像。它們可以做自己喜歡的事。它們當然可以這樣做。哈囉，好孩子！」

「哈囉！」男孩回應他。

「你知道隔兩條街的街角有間家禽店吧？」史顧己問。

「當然知道。」男孩答道。

「聰明的小孩！」史顧己說，「真是個出色的孩子。你知不知道他們店鋪掛的那隻得獎的火雞賣掉了沒？不是那些拿安慰獎的火雞，是得大獎的那隻唷！」

「啥？是那隻跟我一樣大的火雞嗎？」男孩回答。

「多麼討人喜愛的男孩啊！」史顧己說，「跟他談話真令人開心。是的，孩子！」

「牠現在還掛在那呢！」男孩回答。

「是嗎？」史顧己說，「那去幫我買下牠吧。」

「騙人！」男孩嚷道。

「不，不！」史顧己說，「我是認真的。去幫我買下牠，叫他們拿來這裡，我會告訴他們要送到哪裡去。帶夥計過來，我就給你一先令。如果你五分鐘內就能帶他過來，那我就給你半克朗。」

　　男孩像子彈一樣衝了出去。他一定經常練習才能夠跑得像子彈飛射那麼快。

　　「我要把火雞送給克勞契一家！」史顧己搓搓手，喃喃自語道，然後又迸出笑聲，「他不會知道是誰送的，這火雞可有小提姆的兩倍大呢。連喬‧米勒也沒開過這種玩笑呢！」

　　他寫住址的時候手不停地發抖，不過他還是寫好了，然後下樓打開門等著家禽店的夥計到來。當他站在那裡等待時，門環突然吸引住他的目光。

　　「只要我活著，我就會好好珍惜它！」史顧己用手輕拍門環叫道，「我以前根本沒多加注意，它臉上的表情多麼坦率啊！這真是個神奇的門環。啊，火雞來囉！哈囉！萬歲！你好嗎？聖誕快樂！」

　　是那隻火雞！牠一定從來沒用雙腳站立過，否則，牠的腿恐怕不到一分鐘，就像封蠟棒一樣折斷啦。

　　「天啊，扛著這隻火雞到康登鎮真是不可能的任務，」史顧己說，「你一定要有輛馬車。」

　　他呵呵笑著說出這些話，笑著付了火雞的帳，笑著付費給馬車，也笑著獎賞男孩，然後，他再度喘著氣在椅子上坐下來，不停地笑著，直到眼淚流出。

　　刮鬍子可不是件簡單的任務，因為他的手抖得厲害。而且，刮鬍子須精神專注，就算沒有手舞足蹈地動也不行。不過，即便他將鼻子給削下來了，他也會貼上一塊膠布，依舊心滿意足。

　　他穿上最好的衣服，終於上街了。就如同他與現在的耶誕精靈在一起時所見到的，此刻人潮洶湧。史顧己背著手散步，笑容滿面地打量每個人。總而言之，他看起來如此討人喜歡，三四個神情愉快的人忍不住對他說：「先生，早安！聖誕快樂！」後來史顧己還常說，在他所聽過的愉快聲音裡頭，這些是最讓他高興的。

　　他並沒走多遠，因為他看到了一位魁梧的紳士走向他，正是昨日到他的帳房來說「我想，這就是『史顧己與馬利』」的那個紳士。想到他們相遇時，這個老紳士會怎麼看他，史顧己忽然一陣心痛。但他知道現在該怎麼做。

　　「親愛的先生，」史顧己加快腳步，兩手握住老紳士的手說道：「你好嗎？但願你昨天有很大的收獲。你非常地仁慈。先生，祝你聖誕快樂！」

　　「史顧己先生？」

　　「是的，」史顧己說，「正是我本人，我想對你來說這並不是什麼讓人高興的名字。但是，我要請求你的寬恕。不知你是否……」史顧己湊到那位先生耳邊低聲說話。

　　「上帝保佑！」那位先生彷彿喘不過氣似地叫了起來：

「親愛的史顧己先生，你是認真的嗎？」

「如果你樂意的話，」史顧己說，「一毛都不會少。裡面包含了許多拖欠的費用，我保證。你願意幫我這個忙嗎？」

「親愛的先生，」那位紳士握著史顧己的手說道，「我真不知道該說什麼……」

「你什麼都別說了。」史顧己回答，「來見我吧。你會來見我嗎？」

「會的！」老紳士叫道，而且他顯然一定會這麼做。

「謝謝你。」史顧己說，「非常感激，很感謝你。上帝保佑你！」

史顧己上了教堂，又到街上四處閒逛。他看著來來往往的人潮，有時摸摸孩童的頭，有時又問候關懷乞丐，一會兒望向人家屋裡的廚房，一會兒則看看別人家的窗戶，並且發現一切事物居然都能令他感到快樂。他從未想過散步——或是做任何事——可以為自己帶來這麼多快樂。到了下午，他往外甥的家走去。

他在門前徘徊了不下數十次，才終於鼓起勇氣上前敲門，不過他是用衝的。

「親愛的，妳的主人在家嗎？」史顧己對一個漂亮的女孩說道，一個很漂亮的女孩子！

「在，先生。」

「親愛的，他在哪兒呢？」史顧己問。

「他跟太太在餐廳裡。如果您願意，我可以領您進去。」

「謝謝。他認識我的，」史顧己說著，手已經放在餐廳的門把上，「親愛的，我自己進去。」

他輕輕地轉開門把，側著臉探頭進去。裡面的人正盯著已經擺滿食物的餐桌；那些年輕的主婦在此時總是很挑剔，不時要查看一切是否就緒。

「弗瑞德！」史顧己說。

史顧己的外甥媳吃了一驚！史顧己一時忘記她正坐在旁邊的凳子上，否則他無論如何也不會這麼做的。

「我的天哪！」弗瑞德叫道，「看看是誰來了？」

「是我，你的舅舅史顧己。我來與你們共用晚餐。弗瑞德，我可以進來嗎？」

只是讓他進來？他的手沒被握斷就算幸運的了。不到五分鐘，他就有賓至如歸的感覺。沒人比史顧己的外甥更親切熱誠了，他的外甥媳也一樣。塔普來時也展現了同樣的熱情。那個胖妹妹來了也是無比熱情。每個人都來了，也是同樣親切。美好的聚會，很棒的遊戲，美妙的和諧，無比的快樂幸福！

但是，史顧己隔天還是一早就到了辦公室。噢，他好早就到了。他心裡盤算著：如果他第一個到，就能捉住鮑勃克勞契上班遲到的小辮子囉。

他成功了，是的，他成功了！鐘敲了九下也不見鮑勃的

身影。十五分鐘過去了，仍不見鮑勃的身影。鮑勃已經整整遲了十八分三十秒啦。史顧已敞開門坐在帳房內，這樣鮑勃進入小房間時他才看得到。

鮑勃還沒進門就取下了帽子跟圍巾。他瞬間就坐到板凳上，筆飛快地動了起來，好似要試著彌補遲到的過失。

「哈囉！」史顧已盡可能地裝出平日的聲音咆哮道：「你今天這麼晚才來是什麼意思？」

「老闆，我很抱歉，」鮑勃說，「我遲到了。」

「你遲到了？」史顧已重複他的話，「是啊，我想你遲到了。麻煩過來一下。」

「老闆，一年只有這麼一次，」鮑勃從小房間走過來求情道：「我不會再犯了。老闆，我昨晚玩得太高興了。」

「現在，親愛的朋友，我要告訴你，我不能再忍受這樣的事情了。所以，」史顧已從凳子上起身，往鮑勃的腰際一推，使他又搖搖撞撞地晃回小房間，接著又說道：「所以，我要幫你加薪。」

鮑勃全身發抖，不禁往桌上的直尺挪近了些。他剎那間產生一個念頭，想拿直尺往史顧已的腦袋敲下去，再到巷子裡求助，請他們拿一件綁瘋子用的緊身衣過來。

「鮑勃，聖誕快樂！」史顧已帶著一種認真的神情說道，並拍了拍鮑勃的背，「鮑勃，我親愛的夥伴，我要給你一個這麼多年來最快樂的聖誕節！我要幫你加薪，還要盡量幫助你辛苦的家人。今天下午我們再一邊喝著熱騰騰的香甜

果子酒慶祝聖誕，一邊來討論你的問題吧，鮑勃！先把火生起來，再去買一籠煤炭，然後再去做你的事吧，鮑勃克勞契！」

史顧己做得比說得還要好。他一切都履行了，甚至還做得更多。他成了小提姆——他並沒有死——的教父。他成了一個好朋友、好老闆、好人，這個古老的倫敦城，或是這個古老世界裡的任何古老城鎮，都知道他是個好人。有些人嘲笑他的轉變，但史顧己任由他們嘲弄，甚少多加理會。因為他很聰明地知道，這個地球上所發生的一切好事，一開始總會受到某些人的嘲笑；而他也知道，這些人都是很盲目的，盲人笑謎了眼的模樣，總要比其他不討喜的模樣來得好多了。總之，他的心會微笑，這就夠了。

他再也沒和精靈打過交道，此後也滴酒不沾。不過一提到他，大家都會說：任何人都知道，史顧己是最會過聖誕節的人。希望我們大家都是這樣！最後，引用一句小提姆的話：「願上帝保佑我們，保佑我們每一個人！」

A Christmas Carol

By Charles Dickens

PREFACE

I HAVE endeavoured in this Ghostly little book, to raise the Ghost of an Idea, which shall not put my readers out of humour with themselves, with each other, with the season, or with me. May it haunt their houses pleasantly, and no one wish to lay it.

Their faithful Friend and Servant,
C. D.
December, 1843.

STAVE I

MARLEY'S GHOST

MARLEY was dead: to begin with. There is no doubt whatever about that. The register of his burial was signed by the clergyman, the clerk, the undertaker, and the chief mourner. Scrooge signed it: and Scrooge's name was good upon 'Change, for anything he chose to put his hand to. Old Marley was as dead as a door-nail.

Mind! I don't mean to say that I know, of my own knowledge, what there is particularly dead about a door-nail. I might have been inclined, myself, to regard a coffin-nail as the deadest piece of ironmongery in the trade. But the wisdom of our ancestors is in the simile; and my unhallowed hands shall not disturb it, or the Country's done for. You will therefore permit me to repeat, emphatically, that Marley was as dead as a door-nail.

Scrooge knew he was dead? Of course he did. How could it be otherwise? Scrooge and he were partners for I don't know how many years. Scrooge was his sole executor, his sole administrator, his sole assign, his sole residuary legatee, his sole friend, and sole mourner. And even Scrooge was not so dreadfully cut up by the sad event, but that he was an excellent man of business on the very

day of the funeral, and solemnised it with an undoubted bargain.

The mention of Marley's funeral brings me back to the point I started from. There is no doubt that Marley was dead. This must be distinctly understood, or nothing wonderful can come of the story I am going to relate. If we were not perfectly convinced that Hamlet's Father died before the play began, there would be nothing more remarkable in his taking a stroll at night, in an easterly wind, upon his own ramparts, than there would be in any other middle-aged gentleman rashly turning out after dark in a breezy spot—say Saint Paul's Churchyard for instance—literally to astonish his son's weak mind.

Scrooge never painted out Old Marley's name. There it stood, years afterwards, above the warehouse door: Scrooge and Marley. The firm was known as Scrooge and Marley. Sometimes people new to the business called Scrooge Scrooge, and sometimes Marley, but he answered to both names. It was all the same to him.

Oh! But he was a tight-fisted hand at the grind-stone, Scrooge! a squeezing, wrenching, grasping, scraping, clutching, covetous, old sinner! Hard and sharp as flint, from which no steel had ever struck out generous fire; secret, and self-contained, and solitary as an oyster. The cold within him froze his old features, nipped his pointed nose, shrivelled his cheek, stiffened his gait; made his eyes red, his thin lips blue; and spoke out shrewdly in his grating voice. A frosty rime was on his head, and on his eyebrows,

and his wiry chin. He carried his own low temperature always
about with him; he iced his office in the dog-days; and didn't thaw
it one degree at Christmas.

External heat and cold had little influence on Scrooge. No
warmth could warm, no wintry weather chill him. No wind that
blew was bitterer than he, no falling snow was more intent upon
its purpose, no pelting rain less open to entreaty. Foul weather
didn't know where to have him. The heaviest rain, and snow, and
hail, and sleet, could boast of the advantage over him in only one

respect. They often "came down" handsomely, and Scrooge never did.

Nobody ever stopped him in the street to say, with gladsome looks, "My dear Scrooge, how are you? When will you come to see me?" No beggars implored him to bestow a trifle, no children asked him what it was o'clock, no man or woman ever once in all his life inquired the way to such and such a place, of Scrooge. Even the blind men's dogs appeared to know him; and when they saw him coming on, would tug their owners into doorways and up courts; and then would wag their tails as though they said, "No eye at all is better than an evil eye, dark master!"

But what did Scrooge care! It was the very thing he liked. To edge his way along the crowded paths of life, warning all human sympathy to keep its distance, was what the knowing ones call "nuts" to Scrooge.

Once upon a time—of all the good days in the year, on Christmas Eve—old Scrooge sat busy in his counting-house. It was cold, bleak, biting weather: foggy withal: and he could hear the people in the court outside, go wheezing up and down, beating their hands upon their breasts, and stamping their feet upon the pavement stones to warm them. The city clocks had only just gone three, but it was quite dark already—it had not been light all day—and candles were flaring in the windows of the neighbouring offices, like ruddy smears upon the palpable brown air. The fog came pouring in at every chink and keyhole, and was so dense

without, that although the court was of the narrowest, the houses opposite were mere phantoms. To see the dingy cloud come drooping down, obscuring everything, one might have thought that Nature lived hard by, and was brewing on a large scale.

The door of Scrooge's counting-house was open that he might keep his eye upon his clerk, who in a dismal little cell beyond, a sort of tank, was copying letters. Scrooge had a very small fire, but the clerk's fire was so very much smaller that it looked like one coal. But he couldn't replenish it, for Scrooge kept the coal-box in his own room; and so surely as the clerk came in with the shovel, the master predicted that it would be necessary for them to part. Wherefore the clerk put on his white comforter, and tried to warm himself at the candle; in which effort, not being a man of a strong imagination, he failed.

"A merry Christmas, uncle! God save you!" cried a cheerful voice. It was the voice of Scrooge's nephew, who came upon him so quickly that this was the first intimation he had of his approach.

"Bah!" said Scrooge, "Humbug!"

He had so heated himself with rapid walking in the fog and frost, this nephew of Scrooge's, that he was all in a glow; his face was ruddy and handsome; his eyes sparkled, and his breath smoked again.

"Christmas a humbug, uncle!" said Scrooge's nephew. "You don't mean that, I am sure?"

"I do," said Scrooge. "Merry Christmas! What right have you

耕.2002.06.

to be merry? What reason have you to be merry? You're poor enough."

"Come, then," returned the nephew gaily. "What right have you to be dismal? What reason have you to be morose? You're rich enough."

Scrooge having no better answer ready on the spur of the moment, said, "Bah!" again; and followed it up with "Humbug."

"Don't be cross, uncle!" said the nephew.

"What else can I be," returned the uncle, "when I live in such a world of fools as this? Merry Christmas! Out upon merry Christmas! What's Christmas time to you but a time for paying bills without money; a time for finding yourself a year older, but not an hour richer; a time for balancing your books and having every item in 'em through a round dozen of months presented dead against you? If I could work my will," said Scrooge indignantly, "every idiot who goes about with 'Merry Christmas' on his lips, should be boiled with his own pudding, and buried with a stake of holly through his heart. He should!"

"Uncle!" pleaded the nephew.

"Nephew!" returned the uncle sternly, "keep Christmas in your own way, and let me keep it in mine."

"Keep it!" repeated Scrooge's nephew. "But you don't keep it."

"Let me leave it alone, then," said Scrooge. "Much good may it do you! Much good it has ever done you!"

"There are many things from which I might have derived good, by which I have not profited, I dare say," returned the nephew. "Christmas among the rest. But I am sure I have always thought of Christmas time, when it has come round—apart from the veneration due to its sacred name and origin, if anything belonging to it can be apart from that—as a good time; a kind, forgiving, charitable, pleasant time; the only time I know of, in the long calendar of the year, when men and women seem by one consent to open their shut-up hearts freely, and to think of people below them as if they really were fellow-passengers to the grave, and not another race of creatures bound on other journeys. And therefore, uncle, though it has never put a scrap of gold or silver in my pocket, I believe that it has done me good, and will do me good; and I say, God bless it!"

The clerk in the Tank involuntarily applauded. Becoming immediately sensible of the impropriety, he poked the fire, and extinguished the last frail spark for ever.

"Let me hear another sound from you," said Scrooge, "and you'll keep your Christmas by losing your situation! You're quite a powerful speaker, sir," he added, turning to his nephew. "I wonder you don't go into Parliament."

"Don't be angry, uncle. Come! Dine with us to-morrow."

Scrooge said that he would see him—yes, indeed he did. He went the whole length of the expression, and said that he would see him in that extremity first.

"But why?" cried Scrooge's nephew. "Why?"

"Why did you get married?" said Scrooge.

"Because I fell in love."

"Because you fell in love!" growled Scrooge, as if that were the only one thing in the world more ridiculous than a merry Christmas. "Good afternoon!"

"Nay, uncle, but you never came to see me before that happened. Why give it as a reason for not coming now?"

"Good afternoon," said Scrooge.

"I want nothing from you; I ask nothing of you; why cannot we be friends?"

"Good afternoon," said Scrooge.

"I am sorry, with all my heart, to find you so resolute. We have never had any quarrel, to which I have been a party. But I have made the trial in homage to Christmas, and I'll keep my Christmas humour to the last. So A Merry Christmas, uncle!"

"Good afternoon!" said Scrooge.

"And A Happy New Year!"

"Good afternoon!" said Scrooge.

His nephew left the room without an angry word, notwithstanding. He stopped at the outer door to bestow the greetings of the season on the clerk, who, cold as he was, was warmer than Scrooge; for he returned them cordially.

"There's another fellow," muttered Scrooge; who overheard him: "my clerk, with fifteen shillings a week, and a wife and family, talking about a merry Christmas. I'll retire to Bedlam."

This lunatic, in letting Scrooge's nephew out, had let two other people in. They were portly gentlemen, pleasant to behold, and now stood, with their hats off, in Scrooge's office. They had books and papers in their hands, and bowed to him.

"Scrooge and Marley's, I believe," said one of the gentlemen, referring to his list. "Have I the pleasure of addressing Mr. Scrooge, or Mr. Marley?"

"Mr. Marley has been dead these seven years," Scrooge replied. "He died seven years ago, this very night."

"We have no doubt his liberality is well represented by his surviving partner," said the gentleman, presenting his credentials.

It certainly was; for they had been two kindred spirits. At the ominous word "liberality," Scrooge frowned, and shook his head, and handed the credentials back.

"At this festive season of the year, Mr. Scrooge," said the gentleman, taking up a pen, "it is more than usually desirable that we should make some slight provision for the Poor and destitute, who suffer greatly at the present time. Many thousands are in want of common necessaries; hundreds

of thousands are in want of common comforts, sir."

"Are there no prisons?" asked Scrooge.

"Plenty of prisons," said the gentleman, laying down the pen again.

"And the Union workhouses?" demanded Scrooge. "Are they still in operation?"

"They are. Still," returned the gentleman, "I wish I could say they were not."

"The Treadmill and the Poor Law are in full vigour, then?" said Scrooge.

"Both very busy, sir."

"Oh! I was afraid, from what you said at first, that something had occurred to stop them in their useful course," said Scrooge. "I'm very glad to hear it."

"Under the impression that they scarcely furnish Christian cheer of mind or body to the multitude," returned the gentleman, "a few of us are endeavouring to raise a fund to buy the Poor some meat and drink, and means of warmth. We choose this time, because it is a time, of all others, when Want is keenly felt, and Abundance rejoices. What shall I put you down for?"

"Nothing!" Scrooge replied.

"You wish to be anonymous?"

"I wish to be left alone," said Scrooge. "Since you ask me what I wish, gentlemen, that is my answer. I don't make merry myself at Christmas and I can't afford to make idle people merry.

I help to support the establishments I have mentioned—they cost enough; and those who are badly off must go there."

"Many can't go there; and many would rather die."

"If they would rather die," said Scrooge, "they had better do it, and decrease the surplus population. Besides—excuse me—I don't know that."

"But you might know it," observed the gentleman.

"It's not my business," Scrooge returned. "It's enough for a man to understand his own business, and not to interfere with other people's. Mine occupies me constantly. Good afternoon, gentlemen!"

Seeing clearly that it would be useless to pursue their point, the gentlemen withdrew. Scrooge resumed his labours with an improved opinion of himself, and in a more facetious temper than was usual with him.

Meanwhile the fog and darkness thickened so, that people ran about with flaring links, proffering their services to go before horses in carriages, and conduct them on their way. The ancient tower of a church, whose gruff old bell was always peeping slily down at Scrooge out of a Gothic window in the wall, became invisible, and struck the hours and quarters in the clouds, with tremulous vibrations afterwards as if its teeth were chattering in its frozen head up there. The cold became intense. In the main street, at the corner of the court, some labourers were repairing the gas-pipes, and had lighted a great fire in a brazier, round which

a party of ragged men and boys were gathered: warming their hands and winking their eyes before the blaze in rapture. The water-plug being left in solitude, its overflowings sullenly congealed, and turned to misanthropic ice. The brightness of the shops where holly sprigs and berries crackled in the lamp heat of the windows, made pale faces ruddy as they passed. Poulterers' and grocers' trades became a splendid joke: a glorious pageant, with which it was next to impossible to believe that such dull

principles as bargain and sale had anything to do. The Lord Mayor, in the stronghold of the mighty Mansion House, gave orders to his fifty cooks and butlers to keep Christmas as a Lord Mayor's household should; and even the little tailor, whom he had fined five shillings on the previous Monday for being drunk and bloodthirsty in the streets, stirred up to-morrow's pudding in his garret, while his lean wife and the baby sallied out to buy the beef.

Foggier yet, and colder. Piercing, searching, biting cold. If the good Saint Dunstan had but nipped the Evil Spirit's nose with a touch of such weather as that, instead of using his familiar weapons, then indeed he would have roared to lusty purpose. The owner of one scant young nose, gnawed and mumbled by the hungry cold as bones are gnawed by dogs, stooped down at Scrooge's keyhole to regale him with a Christmas carol: but at the first sound of

"God bless you, merry gentleman!
May nothing you dismay!"

Scrooge seized the ruler with such energy of action, that the singer fled in terror, leaving the keyhole to the fog and even more congenial frost.

At length the hour of shutting up the counting-house arrived. With an ill-will Scrooge dismounted from his stool, and tacitly admitted the fact to the expectant clerk in the Tank, who instantly snuffed his candle out, and put on his hat.

"You'll want all day to-morrow, I suppose?" said Scrooge.

"If quite convenient, sir."

"It's not convenient," said Scrooge, "and it's not fair. If I was to stop half-a-crown for it, you'd think yourself ill-used, I'll be bound?"

The clerk smiled faintly.

"And yet," said Scrooge, "you don't think me ill-used, when I pay a day's wages for no work."

The clerk observed that it was only once a year.

"A poor excuse for picking a man's pocket every twenty-fifth of December!" said Scrooge, buttoning his great-coat to the chin. "But I suppose you must have the whole day. Be here all the

earlier next morning."

The clerk promised that he would; and Scrooge walked out with a growl. The office was closed in a twinkling, and the clerk, with the long ends of his white comforter dangling below his waist (for he boasted no great-coat), went down a slide on Cornhill, at the end of a lane of boys, twenty times, in honour of its being Christmas Eve, and then ran home to Camden Town as hard as he could pelt, to play at blindman's-buff.

Scrooge took his melancholy dinner in his usual melancholy tavern; and having read all the newspapers, and beguiled the rest of the evening with his banker's-book, went home to bed. He lived in chambers which had once belonged to his deceased partner. They were a gloomy suite of rooms, in a lowering pile of building up a yard, where it had so little business to be, that one could scarcely help fancying it must have run there when it was a young house, playing at hide-and-seek with other houses, and forgotten the way out again. It was old enough now, and dreary enough, for nobody lived in it but Scrooge, the other rooms being all let out as offices. The yard was so dark that even Scrooge, who knew its every stone, was fain to grope with his hands. The fog and frost so hung about the black old gateway of the house, that it seemed as if the Genius of the Weather sat in mournful meditation on the threshold.

Now, it is a fact, that there was nothing at all particular about the knocker on the door, except that it was very large. It is also a fact, that Scrooge had seen it, night and morning, during his whole residence in that place; also that Scrooge had as little of what is called fancy about him as any man in the city of London, even including—which is a bold word—the corporation, aldermen, and livery. Let it also be borne in mind that Scrooge had not bestowed one thought on Marley, since his last mention of his seven years' dead partner that afternoon. And then let any man explain to me, if he can, how it happened that Scrooge, having his key in the lock of the door, saw in the knocker, without its undergoing any intermediate process of change—not a knocker, but Marley's face.

Marley's face. It was not in impenetrable shadow as the other objects in the yard were, but had a dismal light about it, like a bad lobster in a dark cellar. It was not angry or ferocious, but looked at Scrooge as Marley used to look: with ghostly spectacles turned up on its ghostly forehead. The hair was curiously stirred, as if by breath or hot air; and, though the eyes were wide open, they were perfectly motionless. That, and its livid colour, made it horrible; but its horror seemed to be in spite of the face and beyond its control, rather than a part of its own expression.

As Scrooge looked fixedly at this phenomenon, it was a knocker again.

To say that he was not startled, or that his blood was not conscious of a terrible sensation to which it had been a stranger from infancy, would be untrue. But he put his hand upon the key he had relinquished, turned it sturdily, walked in, and lighted his

candle.

He did pause, with a moment's irresolution, before he shut the door; and he did look cautiously behind it first, as if he half expected to be terrified with the sight of Marley's pigtail sticking out into the hall. But there was nothing on the back of the door, except the screws and nuts that held the knocker on, so he said "Pooh, pooh!" and closed it with a bang.

The sound resounded through the house like thunder. Every room above, and every cask in the wine-merchant's cellars below, appeared to have a separate peal of echoes of its own. Scrooge was not a man to be frightened by echoes. He fastened the door, and walked across the hall, and up the stairs; slowly too: trimming his candle as he went.

You may talk vaguely about driving a coach-and-six up a good old flight of stairs, or through a bad young Act of Parliament; but I mean to say you might have got a hearse up that staircase, and taken it broadwise, with the splinter-bar towards the wall and the door towards the balustrades: and done it easy. There was plenty of width for that, and room to spare; which is perhaps the reason why Scrooge thought he saw a locomotive hearse going on before him in the gloom. Half-a-dozen gas-lamps out of the street wouldn't have lighted the entry too well, so you may suppose that it was pretty dark with Scrooge's dip.

Up Scrooge went, not caring a button for that. Darkness is cheap, and Scrooge liked it. But before he shut his heavy door, he

walked through his rooms to see that all was right. He had just enough recollection of the face to desire to do that.

Sitting-room, bedroom, lumber-room. All as they should be. Nobody under the table, nobody under the sofa; a small fire in the grate; spoon and basin ready; and the little saucepan of gruel (Scrooge had a cold in his head) upon the hob. Nobody under thebed; nobody in the closet; nobody in his dressing-gown, which was hanging up in a suspicious attitude against the wall. Lumber-room as usual. Old fire-guard, old shoes, two fish-baskets, washing-stand on three legs, and a poker.

Quite satisfied, he closed his door, and locked himself in; double-locked himself in, which was not his custom. Thus secured against surprise, he took off his cravat; put on his dressing-gown and slippers, and his nightcap; and sat down before the fire to take his gruel.

It was a very low fire indeed; nothing on such a bitter night. He was obliged to sit close to it, and brood over it, before he could extract the least sensation of warmth from such a handful of fuel. The fireplace was an old one, built by some Dutch merchant long ago, and paved all round with quaint Dutch tiles, designed to illustrate the Scriptures. There were Cains and Abels, Pharaoh's daughters; Queens of Sheba, Angelic messengers descending through the air on clouds like feather-beds, Abrahams, Belshazzars, Apostles putting off to sea in butter-boats, hundreds of figures to attract his thoughts; and yet that face of Marley,

seven years dead, came like the ancient Prophet's rod, and swallowed up the whole. If each smooth tile had been a blank at first, with power to shape some picture on its surface from the disjointed fragments of his thoughts, there would have been a copy of old Marley's head on every one.

"Humbug!" said Scrooge; and walked across the room.

After several turns, he sat down again. As he threw his head back in the chair, his glance happened to rest upon a bell, a disused bell, that hung in the room, and communicated for some purpose now forgotten with a chamber in the highest story of the building. It was with great astonishment, and with a strange, inexplicable dread, that as he looked, he saw this bell begin to swing. It swung so softly in the outset that it scarcely made a sound; but soon it rang out loudly, and so did every bell in the house.

This might have lasted half a minute, or a minute, but it seemed an hour. The bells ceased as they had begun, together. They were succeeded by a clanking noise, deep down below; as if some person were dragging a heavy chain over the casks in the wine-merchant's cellar. Scrooge then remembered to have heard that ghosts in haunted houses were described as dragging chains.

The cellar-door flew open with a booming sound, and then he heard the noise much louder, on the floors below; then coming up the stairs; then coming straight towards his door.

"It's humbug still!" said Scrooge. "I won't believe it."

His colour changed though, when, without a pause, it came

on through the heavy door, and passed into the room before his eyes. Upon its coming in, the dying flame leaped up, as though it cried, "I know him; Marley's Ghost!" and fell again.

The same face: the very same. Marley in his pigtail, usual waistcoat, tights and boots; the tassels on the latter bristling, like his pigtail, and his coat-skirts, and the hair upon his head. The chain he drew was clasped about his middle. It was long, and wound about him like a tail; and it was made (for Scrooge observed it closely) of cash-boxes, keys, padlocks, ledgers, deeds, and heavy purses wrought in steel. His body was transparent; so that Scrooge, observing him, and looking through his waistcoat, could see the two buttons on his coat behind.

Scrooge had often heard it said that Marley had no bowels, but he had never believed it until now.

No, nor did he believe it even now. Though he looked the phantom through and through, and saw it standing before him; though he felt the chilling influence of its death-cold eyes; and marked the very texture of the folded kerchief bound about its head and chin, which wrapper he had not observed before; he was still incredulous, and fought against his senses.

"How now!" said Scrooge, caustic and cold as ever. "What do you want with me?"

"Much!"—Marley's voice, no doubt about it.

"Who are you?"

"Ask me who I was."

"Who were you then?" said Scrooge, raising his voice. "You're particular, for a shade." He was going to say "to a shade," but substituted this, as more appropriate.

"In life I was your partner, Jacob Marley."

"Can you—can you sit down?" asked Scrooge, looking doubtfully at him.

"I can."

"Do it, then."

Scrooge asked the question, because he didn't know whether a ghost so transparent might find himself in a condition to take a chair; and felt that in the event of its being impossible, it might involve the necessity of an embarrassing explanation. But the ghost sat down on the opposite side of the fireplace, as if he were quite used to it.

"You don't believe in me," observed the Ghost.

"I don't," said Scrooge.

"What evidence would you have of my reality beyond that of your senses?"

"I don't know," said Scrooge.

"Why do you doubt your senses?"

"Because," said Scrooge, "a little thing affects them. A slight disorder of the stomach makes them cheats. You may be an undigested bit of beef, a blot of mustard, a crumb of cheese, a fragment of an underdone potato. There's more of gravy than of grave about you, whatever you are!"

Scrooge was not much in the habit of cracking jokes, nor did he feel, in his heart, by any means waggish then. The truth is, that he tried to be smart, as a means of distracting his own attention, and keeping down his terror; for the spectre's voice disturbed the very marrow in his bones.

To sit, staring at those fixed glazed eyes, in silence for a moment, would play, Scrooge felt, the very deuce with him. There was something very awful, too, in the spectre's being provided with an infernal atmosphere of its own. Scrooge could not feel it himself, but this was clearly the case; for though the Ghost sat perfectly motionless, its hair, and skirts, and tassels, were still agitated as by the hot vapour from an oven.

"You see this toothpick?" said Scrooge, returning quickly to the charge, for the reason just assigned; and wishing, though it were only for a second, to divert the vision's stony gaze from himself.

"I do," replied the Ghost.

"You are not looking at it," said Scrooge.

"But I see it," said the Ghost, "notwithstanding."

"Well!" returned Scrooge, "I have but to swallow this, and be for the rest of my days persecuted by a legion of goblins, all of my own creation. Humbug, I tell you! humbug!"

At this the spirit raised a frightful cry, and shook its chain with such a dismal and appalling noise, that Scrooge held on tight to his chair, to save himself from falling in a swoon. But how much greater was his horror, when the phantom taking off the

bandage round its head, as if it were too warm to wear indoors, its lower jaw dropped down upon its breast!

Scrooge fell upon his knees, and clasped his hands before his face.

"Mercy!" he said. "Dreadful apparition, why do you trouble me?"

"Man of the worldly mind!" replied the Ghost, "do you believe in me or not?"

"I do," said Scrooge. "I must. But why do spirits walk the earth, and why do they come to me?"

"It is required of every man," the Ghost returned, "that the spirit within him should walk abroad among his fellowmen, and travel far and wide; and if that spirit goes not forth in life, it is condemned to do so after death. It is doomed to wander through the world—oh, woe is me!—and witness what it cannot share, but might have shared on earth, and turned to happiness!"

Again the spectre raised a cry, and shook its chain and wrung its shadowy hands.

"You are fettered," said Scrooge, trembling. "Tell me why?"

"I wear the chain I forged in life," replied the Ghost. "I made it link by link, and yard by yard; I girded it on of my own free will, and of my own free will I wore it. Is its pattern strange to you?"

Scrooge trembled more and more.

"Or would you know," pursued the Ghost, "the weight and length of the strong coil you bear yourself? It was full as heavy and as long as this, seven Christmas Eves ago. You have laboured on it, since. It is a ponderous chain!"

Scrooge glanced about him on the floor, in the expectation of finding himself surrounded by some fifty or sixty fathoms of iron cable: but he could see nothing.

"Jacob," he said, imploringly. "Old Jacob Marley, tell me more. Speak comfort to me, Jacob!"

"I have none to give," the Ghost replied. "It comes from other regions, Ebenezer Scrooge, and is conveyed by other ministers, to other kinds of men. Nor can I tell you what I would. A very little more is all permitted to me. I cannot rest, I cannot stay, I cannot linger anywhere. My spirit never walked beyond our counting-house—mark me!—in life my spirit never roved beyond the narrow limits of our money-changing hole; and weary journeys lie before me!"

It was a habit with Scrooge, whenever he became thoughtful, to put his hands in his breeches pockets. Pondering on what the Ghost had said, he did so now, but without lifting up his eyes, or getting off his knees.

"You must have been very slow about it, Jacob," Scrooge observed, in a business-like manner, though with humility and deference.

"Slow!" the Ghost repeated.

"Seven years dead," mused Scrooge. "And travelling all the time!"

"The whole time," said the Ghost. "No rest, no peace. Incessant torture of remorse."

"You travel fast?" said Scrooge.

"On the wings of the wind," replied the Ghost.

"You might have got over a great quantity of ground in seven years," said Scrooge.

The Ghost, on hearing this, set up another cry, and clanked its chain so hideously in the dead silence of the night, that the Ward would have been justified in indicting it for a nuisance.

"Oh! captive, bound, and double-ironed," cried the phantom, "not to know, that ages of incessant labour by immortal creatures, for this earth must pass into eternity before the good of which it is susceptible is all developed. Not to know that any Christian spirit working kindly in its little sphere, whatever it may be, will find its mortal life too short for its vast means of usefulness. Not to know that no space of regret can make amends for one life's opportunity misused! Yet such was I! Oh! such was I!"

"But you were always a good man of business, Jacob," faltered Scrooge, who now began to apply this to himself.

"Business!" cried the Ghost, wringing its hands again. "Mankind was my business. The common welfare was my business; charity, mercy, forbearance, and benevolence, were, all, my business. The dealings of my trade were but a drop of water in the comprehensive ocean of my business!"

It held up its chain at arm's length, as if that were the cause

of all its unavailing grief, and flung it heavily upon the ground again.

"At this time of the rolling year," the spectre said, "I suffer most. Why did I walk through crowds of fellow-beings with my eyes turned down, and never raise them to that blessed Star which led the Wise Men to a poor abode! Were there no poor homes to which its light would have conducted me!"

Scrooge was very much dismayed to hear the spectre going on at this rate, and began to quake exceedingly.

"Hear me!" cried the Ghost. "My time is nearly gone."

"I will," said Scrooge. "But don't be hard upon me! Don't be flowery, Jacob! Pray!"

"How it is that I appear before you in a shape that you can see, I may not tell. I have sat invisible beside you many and many a day."

It was not an agreeable idea. Scrooge shivered, and wiped the perspiration from his brow.

"That is no light part of my penance," pursued the Ghost. "I am here to-night to warn you, that you have yet a chance and hope of escaping my fate. A chance and hope of my procuring, Ebenezer."

"You were always a good friend to me," said Scrooge. "Thank'ee!"

"You will be haunted," resumed the Ghost, "by Three Spirits."

Scrooge's countenance fell almost as low as the Ghost's had done.

"Is that the chance and hope you mentioned, Jacob?" he demanded, in a faltering voice.

"It is."

"I—I think I'd rather not," said Scrooge.

"Without their visits," said the Ghost, "you cannot hope to shun the path I tread. Expect the first to-morrow, when the bell tolls One."

"Couldn't I take 'em all at once, and have it over, Jacob?" hinted Scrooge.

"Expect the second on the next night at the same hour. The third upon the next night when the last stroke of Twelve has ceased to vibrate. Look to see me no more; and look that, for your own sake, you remember what has passed between us!"

When it had said these words, the spectre took its wrapper from the table, and bound it round its head, as before. Scrooge knew this, by the smart sound its teeth made, when the jaws were brought together by the bandage. He ventured to raise his eyes again, and found his supernatural visitor confronting him in an erect attitude, with its chain wound over and about its arm.

The apparition walked backward from him; and at every step it took, the window raised itself a little, so that when the spectre reached it, it was wide open.

It beckoned Scrooge to approach, which he did. When they

were within two paces of each other, Marley's Ghost held up its hand, warning him to come no nearer. Scrooge stopped.

Not so much in obedience, as in surprise and fear: for on the raising of the hand, he became sensible of confused noises in the air; incoherent sounds of lamentation and regret; wailings inexpressibly sorrowful and self-accusatory. The spectre, after listening for a moment, joined in the mournful dirge; and floated out upon the bleak, dark night.

Scrooge followed to the window: desperate in his curiosity. He looked out.

The air was filled with phantoms, wandering hither and thither in restless haste, and moaning as they went. Every one of them wore chains like Marley's Ghost; some few (they might be guilty governments) were linked together; none were free. Many had

been personally known to Scrooge in their lives. He had been quite familiar with one old ghost, in a white waistcoat, with a monstrous iron safe attached to its ankle, who cried piteously at being unable to assist a wretched woman with an infant, whom it saw below, upon a door-step. The misery with them all was, clearly, that they sought to interfere, for good, in human matters, and had lost the power for ever.

Whether these creatures faded into mist, or mist enshrouded them, he could not tell. But they and their spirit voices faded together; and the night became as it had been when he walked home.

Scrooge closed the window, and examined the door by which the Ghost had entered. It was double-locked, as he had locked it with his own hands, and the bolts were undisturbed. He tried to say "Humbug!" but stopped at the first syllable. And being, from the emotion he had undergone, or the fatigues of the day, or his glimpse of the Invisible World, or the dull conversation of the Ghost, or the lateness of the hour, much in need of repose; went straight to bed, without undressing, and fell asleep upon the instant.

STAVE II

THE FIRST OF THE THREE SPIRITS

WHEN Scrooge awoke, it was so dark, that looking out of bed, he could scarcely distinguish the transparent window from the opaque walls of his chamber. He was endeavouring to pierce the darkness with his ferret eyes, when the chimes of a neighbouring church struck the four quarters. So he listened for the hour.

To his great astonishment the heavy bell went on from six to seven, and from seven to eight, and regularly up to twelve; then stopped. Twelve! It was past two when he went to bed. The clock was wrong. An icicle must have got into the works. Twelve!

He touched the spring of his repeater, to correct this most preposterous clock. Its rapid little pulse beat twelve: and stopped.

"Why, it isn't possible," said Scrooge, "that I can have slept through a whole day and far into another night. It isn't possible that anything has happened to the sun, and this is twelve at noon!"

The idea being an alarming one, he scrambled out of bed, and groped his way to the window. He was obliged to rub the frost off with the sleeve of his dressing-gown before he could see anything; and could see very little then. All he could make out was, that it was still very foggy and extremely cold, and that there was no noise of people running to and fro, and making a great stir, as there unquestionably would have been if night had beaten off bright day, and taken possession of the world. This was a great relief, because "three days after sight of this First of Exchange pay to Mr. Ebenezer Scrooge or his order," and so forth, would have become a mere United States' security if there were no days to count by.

Scrooge went to bed again, and thought, and thought, and thought it over and over and over, and could make nothing of it. The more he thought, the more perplexed he was; and the more he endeavoured not to think, the more he thought.

Marley's Ghost bothered him exceedingly. Every time he resolved within himself, after mature inquiry, that it was all a dream, his mind flew back again, like a strong spring released, to its first position, and presented the same problem to be worked all through, "Was it a dream or not?"

Scrooge lay in this state until the chime had gone three quarters more, when he remembered, on a sudden, that the Ghost had warned him of a visitation when the bell tolled one. He resolved to lie awake until the hour was passed; and, considering that he could no more go to sleep than go to Heaven, this was perhaps the wisest resolution in his power.

The quarter was so long, that he was more than once

convinced he must have sunk into a doze unconsciously, and missed the clock. At length it broke upon his listening ear.

"Ding, dong!"

"A quarter past," said Scrooge, counting.

"Ding, dong!"

"Half-past!" said Scrooge.

"Ding, dong!"

"A quarter to it," said Scrooge.

"Ding, dong!"

"The hour itself," said Scrooge, triumphantly, "and nothing else!"

He spoke before the hour bell sounded, which it now did with a deep, dull, hollow, melancholy ONE. Light flashed up in the room upon the instant, and the curtains of his bed were drawn.

The curtains of his bed were drawn aside, I tell you, by a hand. Not the curtains at his feet, nor the curtains at his back, but those to which his face was addressed. The curtains of his bed were drawn aside; and Scrooge, starting up into a half-recumbent attitude, found himself face to face with the unearthly visitor who drew them: as close to it as I am now to you, and I am standing in the spirit at your elbow.

It was a strange figure—like a child: yet not so like a child as like an old man, viewed through some supernatural medium, which gave him the appearance of having receded from the view, and being diminished to a child's proportions. Its hair, which hung about its neck and down its back, was white as if with age; and yet the face had not a wrinkle in it, and the tenderest bloom was on the skin. The arms were very long and muscular; the hands the same, as if its hold were of uncommon strength. Its legs and feet, most delicately formed, were, like those upper members, bare. It

wore a tunic of the purest white; and round its waist was bound a lustrous belt, the sheen of which was beautiful. It held a branch of fresh green holly in its hand; and, in singular

contradiction of that wintry emblem, had its dress trimmed with summer flowers. But the strangest thing about it was, that from the crown of its head there sprung a bright clear jet of light, by which all this was visible; and which was doubtless the occasion of its using, in its duller moments, a great extinguisher for a cap, which it now held under its arm.

Even this, though, when Scrooge looked at it with increasing steadiness, was not its strangest quality. For as its belt sparkled and glittered now in one part and now in another, and what was light one instant, at another time was dark, so the figure itself fluctuated in its distinctness: being now a thing with one arm, now with one leg, now with twenty legs, now a pair of legs without a head, now a head without a body: of which dissolving parts, no outline would be visible in the dense gloom wherein they melted away. And in the very wonder of this, it would be itself again; distinct and clear as ever.

"Are you the Spirit, sir, whose coming was foretold to me?" asked Scrooge.

"I am!"

The voice was soft and gentle. Singularly low, as if instead of being so close beside him, it were at a distance.

"Who, and what are you?" Scrooge demanded.

"I am the Ghost of Christmas Past."

"Long Past?" inquired Scrooge: observant of its dwarfish stature.

"No. Your past."

Perhaps, Scrooge could not have told anybody why, if anybody could have asked him; but he had a special desire to see the Spirit in his cap; and begged him to be covered.

"What!" exclaimed the Ghost, "would you so soon put out,

with worldly hands, the light I give? Is it not enough that you are one of those whose passions made this cap, and force me through whole trains of years to wear it low upon my brow!"

Scrooge reverently disclaimed all intention to offend or any knowledge of having wilfully "bonneted" the Spirit at any period of his life. He then made bold to inquire what business brought him there.

"Your welfare!" said the Ghost.

Scrooge expressed himself much obliged, but could not help thinking that a night of unbroken rest would have been more conducive to that end. The Spirit must have heard him thinking, for it said immediately:

"Your reclamation, then. Take heed!"

It put out its strong hand as it spoke, and clasped him gently by the arm.

"Rise! and walk with me!"

It would have been in vain for Scrooge to plead that the weather and the hour were not adapted to pedestrian purposes; that bed was warm, and the thermometer a long way below freezing; that he was clad but lightly in his slippers, dressing-gown, and nightcap; and that he had a cold upon him at that time. The grasp, though gentle as a woman's hand, was not to be resisted. He rose: but finding that the Spirit made towards the window, clasped his robe in supplication.

"I am a mortal," Scrooge remonstrated, "and liable to fall."

"Bear but a touch of my hand there," said the Spirit, laying it upon his heart, "and you shall be upheld in more than this!"

As the words were spoken, they passed through the wall, and stood upon an open country road, with fields on either hand. The city had entirely vanished. Not a vestige of it was to be seen. The darkness and the mist had vanished with it, for it was a clear, cold, winter day, with snow upon the ground.

"Good Heaven!" said Scrooge, clasping his hands together, as he looked about him. "I was bred in this place. I was a boy here!"

The Spirit gazed upon him mildly. Its gentle touch, though it had been light and instantaneous, appeared still present to the old man's sense of feeling. He was conscious of a thousand odours floating in the air, each one connected with a thousand thoughts, and hopes, and joys, and cares long, long, forgotten!

"Your lip is trembling," said the Ghost. "And what is that upon your cheek?"

Scrooge muttered, with an unusual catching in his voice, that it was a pimple; and begged the Ghost to lead him where he would.

"You recollect the way?" inquired the Spirit.

"Remember it!" cried Scrooge with fervour; "I could walk it blindfold."

"Strange to have forgotten it for so many years!" observed the Ghost. "Let us go on."

They walked along the road, Scrooge recognising every gate,

and post, and tree; until a little market-town appeared in the distance, with its bridge, its church, and winding river. Some shaggy ponies now were seen trotting towards them with boys upon their backs, who called to other boys in country gigs and carts, driven by farmers. All these boys were in great spirits, and shouted to each other, until the broad fields were so full of merry music, that the crisp air laughed to hear it!

"These are but shadows of the things that have been," said the Ghost. "They have no consciousness of us."

The jocund travellers came on; and as they came, Scrooge knew and named them every one. Why was he rejoiced beyond all bounds to see them! Why did his cold eye glisten, and his heart leap up as they went past! Why was he filled with gladness when he heard them give each other Merry Christmas, as they parted at cross-roads and bye-ways, for their several homes! What was merry Christmas to Scrooge? Out upon merry Christmas! What good had it ever done to him?

"The school is not quite deserted," said the Ghost. "A solitary child, neglected by his friends, is left there still."

Scrooge said he knew it. And he sobbed.

They left the high-road, by a well-remembered lane, and soon approached a mansion of dull red brick, with a little weathercock-surmounted cupola, on the roof, and a bell hanging in it. It was a large house, but one of broken fortunes; for the spacious offices were little used, their walls were damp and mossy, their windows broken, and their gates decayed. Fowls clucked and strutted in the stables; and the coach-houses and sheds were over-run with grass. Nor was it more retentive of its ancient state, within; for entering the dreary hall, and glancing through the open doors of many rooms, they found them poorly furnished, cold, and vast. There was an earthy savour in the air, a chilly bareness in the place, which associated itself somehow with too much getting up by candle-light, and not too much to eat.

They went, the Ghost and Scrooge, across the hall, to a door at the back of the house. It opened before them, and disclosed a long, bare, melancholy room, made barer still by lines of plain deal forms and desks. At one of these a lonely boy was reading near a feeble fire; and Scrooge sat down upon a form, and wept to see his poor forgotten self as he used to be.

Not a latent echo in the house, not a squeak and scuffle from the mice behind the panelling, not a drip from the half-thawed water-spout in the dull yard behind, not a sigh among the leafless boughs of one despondent poplar, not the idle swinging of an empty store-house door, no, not a clicking in the fire, but fell upon the heart of Scrooge with a softening influence, and gave a freer passage to his tears.

The Spirit touched him on the arm, and pointed to his younger self, intent upon his reading. Suddenly a man, in foreign garments: wonderfully real and distinct to look at: stood outside the window, with an axe stuck in his belt, and leading by the bridle an ass laden with wood.

"Why, it's Ali Baba!" Scrooge exclaimed in ecstasy. "It's dear old honest Ali Baba! Yes, yes, I know! One Christmas time, when yonder solitary child was left here all alone, he did come, for the first time, just like that. Poor boy! And Valentine," said Scrooge, "and his wild brother, Orson; there they go! And what's his name, who was put down in his drawers, asleep, at the Gate of Damascus; don't you see him! And the Sultan's Groom turned upside down by the Genii; there he is upon his head! Serve him

right. I'm glad of it. What business had he to be married to the Princess!"

To hear Scrooge expending all the earnestness of his nature on such subjects, in a most extraordinary voice between laughing and crying; and to see his heightened and excited face; would have been a surprise to his business friends in the city, indeed.

"There's the Parrot!" cried Scrooge. "Green body and yellow tail, with a thing like a lettuce growing out of the top of his head; there he is! Poor Robin Crusoe, he called him, when he came home again after sailing round the island. 'Poor Robin Crusoe, where have you been, Robin Crusoe?' The man thought he was dreaming, but he wasn't. It was the Parrot, you know. There goes Friday, running for his life to the little creek! Halloa! Hoop! Halloo!"

Then, with a rapidity of transition very foreign to his usual character, he said, in pity for his former self, "Poor boy!" and cried again.

"I wish," Scrooge muttered, putting his hand in his pocket, and looking about him, after drying his eyes with his cuff: "but it's too late now."

"What is the matter?" asked the Spirit.

"Nothing," said Scrooge. "Nothing. There was a boy singing a Christmas Carol at my door last night. I should like to have given him something: that's all."

The Ghost smiled thoughtfully, and waved its hand: saying as it did so, "Let us see another Christmas!"

Scrooge's former self grew larger at the words, and the room became a little darker and more dirty. The panels shrunk, the windows cracked; fragments of plaster fell out of the ceiling, and the naked laths were shown instead; but how all this was brought about, Scrooge knew no more than you do. He only knew that it was quite correct; that everything had happened so; that there he was, alone again, when all the other boys had gone home for the jolly holidays.

He was not reading now, but walking up and down despairingly. Scrooge looked at the Ghost, and with a mournful shaking of his head, glanced anxiously towards the door.

It opened; and a little girl, much younger than the boy, came darting in, and putting her arms about his neck, and often kissing him, addressed him as her "Dear, dear brother."

"I have come to bring you home, dear brother!" said the child, clapping her tiny hands, and bending down to laugh. "To bring you home, home, home!"

"Home, little Fan?" returned the boy.

"Yes!" said the child, brimful of glee. "Home, for good and all. Home, for ever and ever. Father is so much kinder

than he used to be, that home's like Heaven! He spoke so gently to me one dear night when I was going to bed, that I was not afraid to ask him once more if you might come home; and he said Yes, you should; and sent me in a coach to bring you. And you're to be a man!" said the child, opening her eyes, "and are never to come back here; but first, we're to be together all the Christmas long, and have the merriest time in all the world."

"You are quite a woman, little Fan!" exclaimed the boy.

She clapped her hands and laughed, and tried to touch his head; but being too little, laughed again, and stood on tiptoe to embrace him. Then she began to drag him, in her childish eagerness, towards the door; and he, nothing loth to go, accompanied her.

A terrible voice in the hall cried, "Bring down Master Scrooge's box, there!" and in the hall appeared the schoolmaster himself, who glared on Master Scrooge with a ferocious condescension, and threw him into a dreadful state of mind by shaking hands with him. He then conveyed him and his sister into the veriest old well of a shivering best-parlour that ever was seen, where the maps upon the wall, and the celestial and terrestrial globes in the windows, were waxy with cold. Here he produced a decanter of curiously light wine, and a block of curiously heavy cake, and administered instalments of those dainties to the young people: at the same time, sending out a meagre servant to offer a glass of "something" to the postboy, who answered that he thanked the gentleman, but if it was the same tap as he had tasted before, he had rather not. Master Scrooge's trunk being by this time tied on to the top of the chaise, the children bade the schoolmaster good-bye right willingly; and getting into it, drove gaily down the garden-sweep: the quick wheels dashing the hoar-frost and snow from off the dark leaves of the evergreens like spray.

"Always a delicate creature, whom a breath might have withered," said the Ghost. "But she had a large heart!"

"So she had," cried Scrooge. "You're right. I will not gainsay it, Spirit. God forbid!"

"She died a woman," said the Ghost, "and had, as I think, children."

"One child," Scrooge returned.

"True," said the Ghost. "Your nephew!"

Scrooge seemed uneasy in his mind; and answered briefly, "Yes."

Although they had but that moment left the school behind them, they were now in the busy thoroughfares of a city, where shadowy passengers passed and repassed; where shadowy carts and coaches battled for the way, and all the strife and tumult of a real city were. It was made plain enough, by the dressing of the shops, that here too it was Christmas time again; but it was evening, and the streets were lighted up.

The Ghost stopped at a certain warehouse door, and asked Scrooge if he knew it.

"Know it!" said Scrooge. "Was I apprenticed here!"

They went in. At sight of an old gentleman in a Welsh wig, sitting behind such a high desk, that if he had been two inches taller he must have knocked his head against the ceiling, Scrooge cried in great excitement:

"Why, it's old Fezziwig! Bless his heart; it's Fezziwig alive again!"

Old Fezziwig laid down his pen, and looked up at the clock, which pointed to the hour of seven. He rubbed his hands; adjusted his capacious waistcoat; laughed all over himself, from his shoes to his organ of benevolence; and called out in a comfortable, oily, rich, fat, jovial voice:

"Yo ho, there! Ebenezer! Dick!"

Scrooge's former self, now grown a young man, came briskly in, accompanied by his fellow-'prentice.

"Dick Wilkins, to be sure!" said Scrooge to the Ghost. "Bless me, yes. There he is. He was very much attached to me, was Dick. Poor Dick! Dear, dear!"

"Yo ho, my boys!" said Fezziwig. "No more work to-night. Christmas Eve, Dick. Christmas, Ebenezer! Let's have the shutters up," cried old Fezziwig, with a sharp clap of his hands, "before a man can say Jack Robinson!"

You wouldn't believe how those two fellows went at it! They charged into the street with the shutters—one, two, three—had 'em up in their places—four, five, six—barred 'em and pinned 'em—seven, eight, nine—and came back before you could have got to twelve, panting like race-horses.

"Hilli-ho!" cried old Fezziwig, skipping down from the high desk, with wonderful agility. "Clear away, my lads, and let's have lots of room here! Hilli-ho, Dick! Chirrup, Ebenezer!"

Clear away! There was nothing they wouldn't have cleared away, or couldn't have cleared away, with old Fezziwig looking on. It was done in a minute. Every movable was packed off, as if it were dismissed from public life for evermore; the floor was swept and watered, the lamps were trimmed, fuel was heaped upon the fire; and the warehouse was as snug, and warm, and dry, and bright a ball-room, as you would desire to see upon a winter's night.

In came a fiddler with a music-book, and went up to the lofty

desk, and made
an orchestra of it, and
tuned like fifty stomach-
aches. In came Mrs. Fezziwig,
one vast substantial smile. In came
the three Miss Fezziwigs, beaming
and lovable. In came the six young
followers whose hearts they broke. In came all the young men and
women employed in the business. In came the housemaid, with
her cousin, the baker. In came the cook, with her brother's
particular friend, the milkman. In came the boy from over the way,
who was suspected of not having board enough from his master;
trying to hide himself behind the girl from next door but one,
who was proved to have had her ears pulled by her mistress. In
they all came, one after another; some shyly, some boldly, some
gracefully, some awkwardly, some pushing, some pulling; in they
all came, anyhow and everyhow. Away they all went, twenty couple

at once; hands half round and back again the other way; down the middle and up again; round and round in various stages of affectionate grouping; old top couple always turning up in the wrong place; new top couple starting off again, as soon as they got there; all top couples at last, and not a bottom one to help them! When this result was brought about, old Fezziwig, clapping his hands to stop the dance, cried out, "Well done!" and the fiddler plunged his hot face into a pot of porter, especially provided for that purpose. But scorning rest, upon his reappearance, he instantly began again, though there were no dancers yet, as if the other fiddler had been carried home, exhausted, on a shutter, and he were a bran-new man resolved to beat him out of sight, or perish.

There were more dances, and there were forfeits, and more dances, and there was cake, and there was negus, and there was a great piece of Cold Roast, and there was a great piece of Cold Boiled, and there were mince-pies, and plenty of beer. But the great effect of the evening came after the Roast and Boiled, when the fiddler (an artful dog, mind! The sort of man who knew his business better than you or I could have told it him!) struck up "Sir Roger de Coverley." Then old Fezziwig stood out to dance with Mrs. Fezziwig. Top couple, too; with a good stiff piece of work cut out for them; three or four and twenty pair of partners; people who were not to be trifled with; people who would dance, and had no notion of walking.

But if they had been twice as many—ah, four times—old Fezziwig would have been a match for them, and so would Mrs. Fezziwig. As to her, she was worthy to be his partner in every sense of the term. If that's not high praise, tell me higher, and I'll use it. A positive light appeared to issue from Fezziwig's calves. They shone in every part of the dance like moons. You couldn't have predicted, at any given time, what would have become of them next. And when old Fezziwig and Mrs. Fezziwig had gone all through the dance; advance and retire, both hands to your partner, bow and curtsey, corkscrew, thread-the-needle, and back again to your place; Fezziwig "cut"—cut so deftly, that he appeared to wink with his legs, and came upon his feet again without a stagger.

When the clock struck eleven, this domestic ball broke up. Mr. and Mrs. Fezziwig took their stations, one on either side of the door, and shaking hands with every person individually as he or she went out, wished him or her a Merry Christmas. When everybody had retired but the two 'prentices, they did the same to them; and thus the cheerful voices died away, and the lads were left to their beds; which were under a counter in the back-shop.

During the whole of this time, Scrooge had acted like a man out of his wits. His heart and soul were in the scene, and with his former self. He corroborated everything, remembered everything, enjoyed everything, and underwent the strangest agitation. It was not until now, when the bright faces of his former self and Dick were turned from them, that he remembered the Ghost, and became conscious that it was looking full upon him, while the light upon its head burnt very clear.

"A small matter," said the Ghost, "to make these silly folks so full of gratitude."

"Small!" echoed Scrooge.

The Spirit signed to him to listen to the two apprentices, who were pouring out their hearts in praise of Fezziwig: and when he had done so, said,

"Why! Is it not? He has spent but a few pounds of your mortal money: three or four perhaps. Is that so much that he deserves this praise?"

"It isn't that," said Scrooge, heated by the remark, and speaking unconsciously like his former, not his latter, self. "It isn't that, Spirit. He has the power to render us happy or unhappy; to make our service light or burdensome; a pleasure or a toil. Say that his power lies in words and looks; in things so slight and insignificant that it is impossible to add and count 'em up: what then? The happiness he gives, is quite as great as if it cost a fortune."

He felt the Spirit's glance, and stopped.

"What is the matter?" asked the Ghost.

"Nothing particular," said Scrooge.

"Something, I think?" the Ghost insisted.

"No," said Scrooge, "No. I should like to be able to say a word or two to my clerk just now. That's all."

His former self turned down the lamps as he gave utterance to the wish; and Scrooge and the Ghost again stood side by side in the open air.

"My time grows short," observed the Spirit. "Quick!"

This was not addressed to Scrooge, or to any one whom he could see, but it produced an immediate effect. For again Scrooge saw himself. He was older now; a man in the prime of life. His face had not the harsh and rigid lines of later years; but it had begun to wear the signs of care and avarice. There was an eager, greedy, restless motion in the eye, which showed the passion that had taken root, and where the shadow of the growing tree would fall.

He was not alone, but sat by the side of a fair young girl in a mourning-dress: in whose eyes there were tears, which sparkled in the light that shone out of the Ghost of Christmas Past.

"It matters little," she said, softly. "To you, very little. Another idol has displaced me; and if it can cheer and comfort you in time to come, as I would have tried to do, I have no just cause to grieve."

"What Idol has displaced you?" he rejoined.

"A golden one."

"This is the even-handed dealing of the world!" he said. "There is nothing on which it is so hard as poverty; and there is nothing it professes to condemn with such severity as the pursuit of wealth!"

"You fear the world too much," she answered, gently. "All your other hopes have merged into the hope of being beyond the chance of its sordid reproach. I have seen your nobler aspirations fall off one by one, until the master-passion, Gain, engrosses you. Have I not?"

"What then?" he retorted. "Even if I have grown so much wiser, what then? I am not changed towards you."

She shook her head.

"Am I?"

"Our contract is an old one. It was made when we were both poor and content to be so, until, in good season, we could improve our worldly fortune by our patient industry. You are changed. When it was made, you were another man."

"I was a boy," he said impatiently.

"Your own feeling tells you that you were not what you are," she returned. "I am. That which promised happiness when we were one in heart, is fraught with misery now that we are two. How often and how keenly I have thought of this, I will not say. It is enough that I have thought of it, and can release you."

"Have I ever sought release?"

"In words. No. Never."

"In what, then?"

"In a changed nature; in an altered spirit; in another atmosphere of life; another Hope as its great end. In everything that made my love of any worth or value in your sight. If this had

never been between us," said the girl, looking mildly, but with steadiness, upon him; "tell me, would you seek me out and try to win me now? Ah, no!"

He seemed to yield to the justice of this supposition, in spite of himself. But he said with a struggle, "You think not."

"I would gladly think otherwise if I could," she answered, "Heaven knows! When I have learned a Truth like this, I know how strong and irresistible it must be. But if you were free to-day, to-morrow, yesterday, can even I believe that you would choose a dowerless girl—you who, in your very confidence with her, weigh everything by Gain: or, choosing her, if for a moment you were false enough to your one guiding principle to do so, do I not know that your repentance and regret would surely follow? I do; and I release you. With a full heart, for the love of him you once were."

He was about to speak; but with her head turned from him, she resumed.

"You may—the memory of what is past half makes me hope you will—have pain in this. A very, very brief time, and you will dismiss the recollection of it, gladly, as an unprofitable dream, from which it happened well that you awoke. May you be happy in the life you have chosen!"

She left him, and they parted.

"Spirit!" said Scrooge, "show me no more! Conduct me home. Why do you delight to torture me?"

"One shadow more!" exclaimed the Ghost.

"No more!" cried Scrooge. "No more. I don't wish to see it. Show me no more!"

But the relentless Ghost pinioned him in both his arms, and forced him to observe what happened next.

They were in another scene and place; a room, not very large or handsome, but full of comfort. Near to the winter fire sat a beautiful young girl, so like that last that Scrooge believed it was the same, until he saw her, now a comely matron, sitting opposite her daughter. The noise in this room was perfectly tumultuous, for there were more children there, than Scrooge in his agitated state of mind could count; and, unlike the celebrated herd in the poem, they were not forty children conducting themselves like one, but every child was conducting itself like forty. The consequences were uproarious beyond belief; but no one seemed to care; on the contrary, the mother and daughter laughed heartily, and enjoyed it very much; and the latter, soon beginning to mingle in the sports, got pillaged by the young brigands most ruthlessly. What would I not have given to be one of them! Though I never could have been so rude, no, no! I wouldn't for the wealth of all the world have crushed that braided hair, and torn it down; and for the precious little shoe, I wouldn't have plucked it off, God bless my soul! To save my life. As to measuring her waist in sport, as they did, bold young brood, I couldn't have done it; I should have expected my arm to have grown round it for a punishment, and never come straight again. And yet I should have dearly liked, I own, to have touched her lips; to have questioned her, that she might have opened them; to have looked upon the lashes of her downcast eyes, and never raised a blush; to have let loose waves of hair, an inch of which would be a keepsake beyond price: in short, I should have liked, I do confess, to have had the lightest licence of a child, and yet to have been man enough to know its value.

But now a knocking at the door was heard, and such a rush immediately ensued that she with laughing face and plundered dress was borne towards it the centre of a flushed and boisterous group, just in time to greet the father, who came home attended

by a man laden with Christmas toys and presents. Then the shouting and the struggling, and the onslaught that was made on the defenceless porter! The scaling him with chairs for ladders to dive into his pockets, despoil him of brown-paper parcels, hold on tight by his cravat, hug him round his neck, pommel his back, and kick his legs in irrepressible affection! The shouts of wonder and delight with which the development of every package was received!

The terrible announcement that the baby had been taken in the act of putting a doll's frying-pan into his mouth, and was more than suspected of having swallowed a fictitious turkey, glued on a wooden platter! The immense relief of finding this a false alarm! The joy, and gratitude, and ecstasy! They are all indescribable alike. It is enough that by degrees the children and their emotions got out of the parlour, and by one stair at a time, up to the top of the house; where they went to bed, and so subsided.

And now Scrooge looked on more attentively than ever, when the master of the house, having his daughter leaning fondly on him, sat down with her and her mother at his own fireside; and when he thought that such another creature, quite as graceful and as full of promise, might have called him father, and been a spring-time in the haggard winter of his life, his sight grew very dim indeed.

"Belle," said the husband, turning to his wife with a smile, "I saw an old friend of yours this afternoon."

"Who was it?"

"Guess!"

"How can I? Tut, don't I know?" she added in the same breath, laughing as he laughed. "Mr. Scrooge."

"Mr. Scrooge it was. I passed his office window; and as it was not shut up, and he had a candle inside, I could scarcely help seeing him. His partner lies upon the point of death, I hear; and there he sat alone. Quite alone in the world, I do believe."

"Spirit!" said Scrooge in a broken voice, "remove me from this place."

"I told you these were shadows of the things that have been," said the Ghost. "That they are what they are, do not blame me!"

"Remove me!" Scrooge exclaimed, "I cannot bear it!"

He turned upon the Ghost, and seeing that it looked upon him with a face, in which in some strange way there were fragments of all the faces it had shown him, wrestled with it.

"Leave me! Take me back. Haunt me no longer!"

In the struggle, if that can be called a struggle in which the Ghost with no visible resistance on its own part was undisturbed by any effort of its adversary, Scrooge observed that its light was burning high and bright; and dimly connecting that with its influence over him, he seized the extinguisher-cap, and by a sudden action pressed it down upon its head.

The Spirit dropped beneath it, so that the extinguisher covered its whole form; but though Scrooge pressed it down with all his force, he could not hide the light: which streamed from under it, in an unbroken flood upon the ground.

He was conscious of being exhausted, and overcome by an irresistible drowsiness; and, further, of being in his own bedroom. He gave the cap a parting squeeze, in which his hand relaxed; and had barely time to reel to bed, before he sank into a heavy sleep.

STAVE III

THE SECOND OF
THE THREE SPIRITS

AWAKING in the middle of a prodigiously tough snore, and sitting up in bed to get his thoughts together, Scrooge had no occasion to be told that the bell was again upon the stroke of One. He felt that he was restored to consciousness in the right nick of time, for the especial purpose of holding a conference with the second messenger despatched to him through Jacob Marley's intervention. But finding that he turned uncomfortably cold when he began to wonder which of his curtains this new spectre would draw back, he put them every one aside with his own hands; and lying down again, established a sharp look-out all round the bed. For he wished to challenge the Spirit on the moment of its appearance, and did not wish to be taken by surprise, and made nervous.

Gentlemen of the free-and-easy sort, who plume themselves on being acquainted with a move or two, and being usually equal to the time-of-day, express the wide range of their capacity for adventure by observing that they are good for anything from pitch-and-toss to manslaughter; between which opposite extremes, no doubt, there lies a tolerably wide and comprehensive range of subjects. Without venturing for Scrooge quite as hardily as this, I don't mind calling on you to believe that he was ready for a good broad field of strange appearances, and that nothing between a baby and rhinoceros would have astonished him very much.

Now, being prepared for almost anything, he was not by any means prepared for nothing; and, consequently, when the Bell struck One, and no shape appeared, he was taken with a violent fit of trembling. Five minutes, ten minutes, a quarter of an hour went by, yet nothing came. All this time, he lay upon his bed, the very core and centre of a blaze of ruddy light, which streamed upon it when the clock proclaimed the hour; and which, being only light, was more alarming than a dozen ghosts, as he was powerless to make out what it meant, or would be at; and was sometimes apprehensive that he might be at that very moment an interesting case of spontaneous combustion, without having the consolation of knowing it. At last, however, he began to think—as you or I would have thought at first; for it is always the person not in the predicament who knows what ought to have been done in it, and would unquestionably have done it too—at last, I say, he began to think that the source and secret of this ghostly light might be in the adjoining room, from whence, on further tracing it, it seemed to shine. This idea taking full possession of his mind, he got up softly and shuffled in his slippers to the door.

The moment Scrooge's hand was on the lock, a strange voice

called him by his name, and bade him enter. He obeyed.

It was his own room. There was no doubt about that. But it had undergone a surprising transformation. The walls and ceiling were so hung with living green, that it looked a perfect grove; from every part of which, bright gleaming berries glistened. The crisp leaves of holly, mistletoe, and ivy reflected back the light, as if so many little mirrors had been scattered there; and such a mighty blaze went roaring up the chimney, as that dull petrification of a hearth had never known in Scrooge's time, or Marley's, or for many and many a winter season gone. Heaped up on the floor, to form a kind of throne, were turkeys, geese, game, poultry, brawn, great joints of meat, sucking-pigs, long wreaths of sausages, mince-pies, plum-puddings, barrels of oysters, red-hot chestnuts, cherry-cheeked apples, juicy oranges, luscious pears, immense twelfth-cakes, and seething bowls of punch, that made the chamber dim with their delicious steam. In easy state upon this couch, there sat a jolly Giant, glorious to see; who bore a glowing torch, in shape not unlike Plenty's horn, and held it up, high up, to shed its light on Scrooge, as he came peeping round the door.

"Come in!" exclaimed the Ghost. "Come in! and know me better, man!"

Scrooge entered timidly, and hung his head before this Spirit. He was not the dogged Scrooge he had been; and though the Spirit's eyes were clear and kind, he did not like to meet them.

"I am the Ghost of Christmas Present," said the Spirit.

"Look upon me!"

Scrooge reverently did so. It was clothed in one simple green robe, or mantle, bordered with white fur. This garment hung so loosely on the figure, that its capacious breast was bare, as if disdaining to be warded or concealed by any artifice. Its feet, observable beneath the ample folds of the garment, were also bare; and on its head it wore no other covering than a holly wreath, set here and there with shining icicles. Its dark brown curls were long and free; free as its genial face, its sparkling eye, its open hand, its cheery voice, its unconstrained demeanour, and its joyful air. Girded round its middle was an antique scabbard; but no sword was in it, and the ancient sheath was eaten up with rust.

"You have never seen the like of me before!" exclaimed the Spirit.

"Never," Scrooge made answer to it.

"Have never walked forth with the younger members of my family; meaning (for I am very young) my elder brothers born in these later years?" pursued the Phantom.

"I don't think I have," said Scrooge. "I am afraid I have not. Have you had many brothers, Spirit?"

"More than eighteen hundred," said the Ghost.

"A tremendous family to provide for!" muttered Scrooge.

The Ghost of Christmas Present rose.

"Spirit," said Scrooge submissively, "conduct me where you will. I went forth last night on compulsion, and I learnt a lesson which is working now. To-night, if you have aught to teach me, let me profit by it."

"Touch my robe!"

Scrooge did as he was told, and held it fast.

Holly, mistletoe, red berries, ivy, turkeys, geese, game, poultry, brawn, meat, pigs, sausages, oysters, pies, puddings, fruit, and punch, all vanished instantly. So did the room, the fire, the ruddy glow, the hour of night, and they stood in the city streets on Christmas morning, where (for the weather was severe) the people made a rough, but brisk and not unpleasant kind of music, in scraping the snow from the pavement in front of their dwellings, and from the tops of their houses, whence it was mad delight to the boys to see it come plumping down into the road below, and splitting into artificial little snow-storms.

The house fronts looked black enough, and the windows blacker, contrasting with the smooth white sheet of snow upon the roofs, and with the dirtier snow upon the ground; which last deposit had been ploughed up in deep furrows by the heavy wheels of carts and waggons; furrows that crossed and re-crossed each other hundreds of times where the great streets branched off; and made intricate channels, hard to trace in the thick yellow mud and icy water. The sky was gloomy, and the shortest streets were choked up with a dingy mist, half thawed, half frozen, whose heavier particles descended in a shower of sooty atoms, as if all the chimneys in Great Britain had, by one consent, caught fire, and were blazing away to their dear hearts' content. There was nothing very cheerful in the climate or the town, and yet was there an air of cheerfulness abroad that the clearest summer air and brightest summer sun might have endeavoured to diffuse in vain.

For, the people who were shovelling away on the housetops were jovial and full of glee; calling out to one another from the parapets, and now and then exchanging a facetious snowball— better-natured missile far than many a wordy jest— laughing heartily if it went right and not less heartily if it went wrong. The poulterers' shops were still half open, and the fruiterers' were radiant in their glory. There were great, round, pot-bellied baskets of chestnuts, shaped like the waistcoats of jolly old gentlemen, lolling at the doors, and tumbling out into the street in their apoplectic opulence. There were ruddy, brown-faced, broad-girthed Spanish Onions, shining in

the fatness of their growth like Spanish Friars, and winking from their shelves in wanton slyness at the girls as they went by, and glanced demurely at the hung-up mistletoe. There were pears and apples, clustered high in blooming pyramids; there were bunches of grapes, made, in the shopkeepers' benevolence to dangle from conspicuous hooks, that people's mouths might water gratis as they passed; there were piles of filberts, mossy and brown, recalling, in their fragrance, ancient walks among the woods, and pleasant shufflings ankle deep through withered leaves; there were Norfolk Biffins, squat and swarthy, setting off the yellow of the oranges and lemons, and, in the great compactness of their juicy persons, urgently entreating and beseeching to be carried home in paper bags and eaten after dinner. The very gold and silver fish, set forth among these choice fruits in a bowl, though members of a dull and stagnant-blooded race, appeared to know that there was something going on; and, to a fish, went gasping round and round their little world in slow and passionless excitement.

The Grocers'! oh, the Grocers'! nearly closed, with perhaps two shutters down, or one; but through those gaps such glimpses! It was not alone that the scales descending on the counter made a merry sound, or that the twine and roller parted company so briskly, or that the canisters were rattled up and down like juggling tricks, or even that the blended scents of tea and coffee were so grateful to the nose, or even that the raisins were so plentiful and rare, the almonds so extremely white, the sticks of cinnamon so long and straight, the other spices so delicious, the candied fruits so caked and spotted with molten sugar as to make the coldest lookers-on feel faint and subsequently bilious. Nor was it that the figs were moist and pulpy, or that the French plums blushed in modest tartness from their highly-decorated boxes, or that everything was good to eat and in its Christmas dress; but the customers were all so hurried and so eager in the hopeful promise of the day, that they tumbled up against each other at the door,

crashing their wicker baskets wildly, and left their purchases upon the counter, and came running back to fetch them, and committed hundreds of the like mistakes, in the best humour possible; while the Grocer and his people were so frank and fresh that the polished hearts with which they fastened their aprons behind might have been their own, worn outside for general inspection, and for Christmas daws to peck at if they chose.

But soon the steeples called good people all, to church and chapel, and away they came, flocking through the streets in their best clothes, and with their gayest faces. And at the same time there emerged from scores of bye-streets, lanes, and nameless turnings, innumerable people, carrying their dinners to the bakers' shops. The sight of these poor revellers appeared to interest the Spirit very much, for he stood with

Scrooge beside him in a baker's doorway, and taking off the covers as their bearers passed, sprinkled incense on their dinners from his torch. And it was a very uncommon kind of torch, for once or twice when there were angry words between some dinner-carriers who had jostled each other, he shed a few drops of water on them from it, and their good humour was restored directly. For they said, it was a shame to quarrel upon Christmas Day. And so it was! God love it, so it was!

In time the bells ceased, and the bakers were shut up; and yet there was a genial shadowing forth of all these dinners and the progress of their cooking, in the thawed blotch of wet above each baker's oven; where the pavement smoked as if its stones were cooking too.

"Is there a peculiar flavour in what you sprinkle from your torch?" asked Scrooge.

"There is. My own."

"Would it apply to any kind of dinner on this day?" asked Scrooge.

"To any kindly given. To a poor one most."

"Why to a poor one most?" asked Scrooge.

"Because it needs it most."

"Spirit," said Scrooge, after a moment's thought, "I wonder you, of all the beings in the many worlds about us, should desire to cramp these people's opportunities of innocent enjoyment."

"I!" cried the Spirit.

"You would deprive them of their means of dining every seventh day, often the only day on which they can be said to dine at all," said Scrooge. "Wouldn't you?"

"I!" cried the Spirit.

"You seek to close these places on the Seventh Day?" said Scrooge. "And it comes to the same thing."

"I seek!" exclaimed the Spirit.

"Forgive me if I am wrong. It has been done in your name, or at least in that of your family," said Scrooge.

"There are some upon this earth of yours," returned the Spirit, "who lay claim to know us, and who do their deeds of passion, pride, ill-will, hatred, envy, bigotry, and selfishness in our name, who are as strange to us and all our kith and kin, as if they had never lived. Remember that, and charge their doings on themselves, not us."

Scrooge promised that he would; and they went on, invisible, as they had been before, into the suburbs of the town. It was a remarkable quality of the Ghost (which Scrooge had observed at the baker's), that notwithstanding his gigantic size, he could accommodate himself to any place with ease; and that he stood beneath a low roof quite as gracefully and like a supernatural creature, as it was possible he could have done in any lofty hall.

And perhaps it was the pleasure the good Spirit had in showing off this power of his, or else it was his own kind, generous, hearty nature, and his sympathy with all poor men, that led him straight to Scrooge's clerk's; for there he went, and took Scrooge with him, holding to his robe; and on the threshold of the door the Spirit smiled, and stopped to bless Bob Cratchit's dwelling with the sprinkling of his torch. Think of that! Bob had but fifteen "Bob" a-week himself; he pocketed on Saturdays but fifteen copies of his Christian name; and yet the Ghost of Christmas Present blessed his four-roomed house!

Then up rose Mrs. Cratchit, Cratchit's wife, dressed out but poorly in a twice-turned gown, but brave in ribbons, which are cheap and make a goodly show for sixpence; and she laid the cloth, assisted by Belinda Cratchit, second of her daughters, also brave in ribbons; while Master Peter Cratchit plunged a fork into the saucepan of potatoes, and getting the corners of his monstrous shirt collar (Bob's private property, conferred upon his son and heir in honour of the day) into his mouth, rejoiced to find himself so gallantly attired, and yearned to show his linen in the fashionable Parks. And now two smaller Cratchits, boy and girl, came tearing in, screaming that outside the baker's they had smelt the goose, and known it for their own; and basking in luxurious thoughts of sage and onion, these young Cratchits danced about the table, and exalted Master Peter Cratchit to the skies, while he (not proud, although his collars nearly choked him) blew the fire, until the slow potatoes bubbling up, knocked loudly at the saucepan-lid to be let out and peeled.

"What has ever got your precious father then?" said Mrs. Cratchit. "And your brother, Tiny Tim! And Martha warn't as late last Christmas Day by half-an-hour?"

"Here's Martha, mother!" said a girl, appearing as she spoke.

"Here's Martha, mother!" cried the two young Cratchits. "Hurrah! There's such a goose, Martha!"

"Why, bless your heart alive, my dear, how late you are!" said Mrs. Cratchit, kissing her a dozen times, and taking off her shawl and bonnet for her with officious zeal.

"We'd a deal of work to finish up last night," replied the girl, "and had to clear away this morning, mother!"

"Well! Never mind so long as you are come," said Mrs.

Cratchit. "Sit ye down before the fire, my dear, and have a warm, Lord bless ye!"

"No, no! There's father coming," cried the two young Cratchits, who were everywhere at once. "Hide, Martha, hide!"

So Martha hid herself, and in came little Bob, the father, with at least three feet of comforter exclusive of the fringe, hanging down before him; and his threadbare clothes darned up and brushed, to look seasonable; and Tiny Tim upon his shoulder. Alas for Tiny Tim, he bore a little crutch, and had his limbs supported by an iron frame!

"Why, where's our Martha?" cried Bob Cratchit, looking

round.

"Not coming," said Mrs. Cratchit.

"Not coming!" said Bob, with a sudden declension in his high spirits; for he had been Tim's blood horse all the way from church, and had come home rampant. "Not coming upon Christmas Day!"

Martha didn't like to see him disappointed, if it were only in joke; so she came out prematurely from behind the closet door, and ran into his arms, while the two young Cratchits hustled Tiny Tim, and bore him off into the wash-house, that he might hear the pudding singing in the copper.

"And how did little Tim behave?" asked Mrs. Cratchit, when she had rallied Bob on his credulity, and Bob had hugged his daughter to his heart's content.

"As good as gold," said Bob, "and better. Somehow he gets thoughtful, sitting by himself so much, and thinks the strangest things you ever heard. He told me, coming home, that he hoped the people saw him in the church, because he was a cripple, and it might be pleasant to them to remember upon Christmas Day, who made lame beggars walk, and blind men see."

Bob's voice was tremulous when he told them this, and trembled more when he said that Tiny Tim was growing strong and hearty.

His active little crutch was heard upon the floor, and back came Tiny Tim before another word was spoken, escorted by his brother and sister to his stool before the fire; and while Bob, turning up his cuffs—as if, poor fellow, they were capable of being made more shabby—compounded some hot mixture in a jug with gin and lemons, and stirred it round and round and put it on the hob to simmer; Master Peter, and the two ubiquitous young Cratchits went to fetch the goose, with which they soon returned in high procession.

Such a bustle ensued that you might have thought a goose the rarest of all birds; a feathered phenomenon, to which a black swan was a matter of course—and in truth it was something very like it in that house. Mrs. Cratchit made the gravy (ready beforehand in a little saucepan) hissing hot; Master Peter mashed the potatoes with incredible vigour; Miss Belinda sweetened up the apple-sauce; Martha dusted the hot plates; Bob took Tiny Tim beside him in a tiny corner at the table; the two young Cratchits set chairs for everybody, not forgetting themselves, and mounting guard upon their posts, crammed spoons into their mouths, lest they should shriek for goose before their turn came to be helped. At last the dishes were set on, and grace was said. It was succeeded by a breathless pause, as Mrs. Cratchit, looking slowly all along the carving-knife, prepared to plunge it in the breast; but when she did, and when the long expected gush of stuffing issued forth, one murmur of delight arose all round the board, and even Tiny Tim, excited by the two young Cratchits, beat on the table with the handle of his knife, and feebly cried Hurrah!

There never was such a goose. Bob said he didn't believe there ever was such a goose cooked. Its tenderness and flavour, size and cheapness, were the themes of universal admiration. Eked out by apple-sauce and mashed potatoes, it was a sufficient dinner for the whole family; indeed, as Mrs. Cratchit said with great delight (surveying one small atom of a bone upon the dish), they hadn't ate it all at last! Yet every one had had enough, and the youngest Cratchits in particular, were steeped in sage and onion to the eyebrows! But now, the plates being changed by Miss Belinda, Mrs. Cratchit left the room alone—too nervous to bear witnesses—to take the pudding up and bring it in.

Suppose it should not be done enough! Suppose it should break in turning out! Suppose somebody should have got over the wall of the back-yard, and stolen it, while they were merry with the goose—a supposition at which the two young Cratchits became livid! All sorts of horrors were supposed.

Hallo! A great deal of steam! The pudding was out of the

copper. A smell like a washing-day! That was the cloth. A smell like an eating-house and a pastrycook's next door to each other, with a laundress's next door to that! That was the pudding! In half a minute Mrs. Cratchit entered—flushed, but smiling proudly—with the pudding, like a speckled cannon-ball, so hard and firm, blazing in half of half-a-quartern of ignited brandy, and bedight with Christmas holly stuck into the top.

Oh, a wonderful pudding! Bob Cratchit said, and calmly too, that he regarded it as the greatest success achieved by Mrs. Cratchit since their marriage. Mrs. Cratchit said that now the weight was off her mind, she would confess she had had her doubts about the quantity of flour. Everybody had something to say about it, but nobody said or thought it was at all a small pudding for a large family. It would have been flat heresy to do so. Any Cratchit would have blushed to hint at such a thing.

At last the dinner was all done, the cloth was cleared, the hearth swept, and the fire made up. The compound in the jug being tasted, and considered perfect, apples and oranges were put upon the table, and a shovel-full of chestnuts on the fire. Then all the Cratchit family drew round the hearth, in what Bob Cratchit called a circle, meaning half a one; and at Bob Cratchit's elbow stood the family display of glass. Two tumblers, and a custard-cup without a handle.

These held the hot stuff from the jug, however, as well as golden goblets would have done; and Bob served it out with beaming looks, while the chestnuts on the fire sputtered and cracked noisily. Then Bob proposed:

"A Merry Christmas to us all, my dears. God bless us!"

Which all the family re-echoed.

"God bless us every one!" said Tiny Tim, the last of all.

He sat very close to his father's side upon his little stool. Bob held his withered little hand in his, as if he loved the child, and wished to keep him by his side, and dreaded that he might be taken from him.

"Spirit," said Scrooge, with an interest he had never felt before, "tell me if Tiny Tim will live."

"I see a vacant seat," replied the Ghost, "in the poor chimney-corner, and a crutch without an owner, carefully preserved. If these shadows remain unaltered by the Future, the child will die."

"No, no," said Scrooge. "Oh, no, kind Spirit! say he will be spared."

"If these shadows remain unaltered by the Future, none other of my race," returned the Ghost, "will find him here. What then? If he be like to die, he had better do it, and decrease the surplus population."

Scrooge hung his head to hear his own words quoted by the Spirit, and was overcome with penitence and grief.

"Man," said the Ghost, "if man you be in heart, not adamant, forbear that wicked cant until you have discovered What the surplus is, and Where it is. Will you decide what men shall live, what men shall die? It may be, that in the sight of Heaven, you are more worthless and less fit to live than millions like this poor man's child. Oh God! to hear the Insect on the leaf pronouncing on the too much life among his hungry brothers in the dust!"

Scrooge bent before the Ghost's rebuke, and trembling cast his eyes upon the ground. But he raised them speedily, on hearing his own name.

"Mr. Scrooge!" said Bob; "I'll give you Mr. Scrooge, the Founder of the Feast!"

"The Founder of the Feast indeed!" cried Mrs. Cratchit, reddening. "I wish I had him here. I'd give him a piece of my mind to feast upon, and I hope he'd have a good appetite for it."

"My dear," said Bob, "the children! Christmas Day."

"It should be Christmas Day, I am sure," said she, "on which one drinks the health of such an odious, stingy, hard, unfeeling man as Mr. Scrooge. You know he is, Robert! Nobody knows it better than you do, poor fellow!"

"My dear," was Bob's mild answer, "Christmas Day."

"I'll drink his health for your sake and the Day's," said Mrs. Cratchit, "not for his. Long life to him! A merry Christmas and a happy new year! He'll be very merry and very happy, I have no doubt!"

The children drank the toast after her. It was the first of their proceedings which had no heartiness. Tiny Tim drank it last of all, but he didn't care twopence for it. Scrooge was the Ogre of the family. The mention of his name cast a dark shadow on the party, which was not dispelled for full five minutes.

After it had passed away, they were ten times merrier than before, from the mere relief of Scrooge the Baleful being done with. Bob Cratchit told them how he had a situation in his eye for Master Peter, which would bring in, if obtained, full five-and-sixpence weekly. The two young Cratchits laughed tremendously at the idea of Peter's being a man of business; and Peter himself looked thoughtfully at the fire from between his collars, as if he were deliberating what particular investments he should favour when he came into the receipt of that bewildering income. Martha, who was a poor apprentice at a milliner's, then told them what kind of work she had to do, and how many hours she worked at a stretch, and how she meant to lie abed to-morrow morning for a good long rest; to-morrow being a holiday she passed at

home. Also how she had seen a countess and a lord some days before, and how the lord "was much about as tall as Peter;" at which Peter pulled up his collars so high that you couldn't have seen his head if you had been there. All this time the chestnuts and the jug went round and round; and by-and-bye they had a song, about a lost child travelling in the snow, from Tiny Tim, who had a plaintive little voice, and sang it very well indeed.

There was nothing of high mark in this. They were not a handsome family; they were not well dressed; their shoes were far from being water-proof; their clothes were scanty; and Peter might have known, and very likely did, the inside of a pawnbroker's. But, they were happy, grateful, pleased with one another, and contented with the time; and when they faded, and looked happier yet in the bright sprinklings of the Spirit's torch at parting, Scrooge had his eye upon them, and especially on Tiny Tim, until the last.

By this time it was getting dark, and snowing pretty heavily; and as Scrooge and the Spirit went along the streets, the brightness of the roaring fires in kitchens, parlours, and all sorts of rooms, was wonderful. Here, the flickering of the blaze showed preparations for a cosy dinner, with hot plates baking through and through before the fire, and deep red curtains, ready to be drawn to shut out cold and darkness. There all the children of the house were running out into the snow to meet their married sisters, brothers, cousins, uncles, aunts, and be the first to greet them. Here, again, were shadows on the window-blind of guests assembling; and there a group of handsome girls, all hooded and fur-booted, and all chattering at once, tripped lightly off to some near neighbour's house; where, woe upon the single man who saw them enter—artful witches, well they knew it—in a glow!

But, if you had judged from the numbers of people on their way to friendly gatherings, you might have thought that no one was at home to give them welcome when they got there, instead of every house expecting company, and piling up its fires half-chimney high. Blessings on it, how the Ghost exulted! How it bared its breadth of breast, and opened its capacious palm, and floated on, outpouring, with a generous hand, its bright and harmless mirth on everything within its reach! The very lamplighter, who ran on before, dotting the dusky street with specks of light, and who was dressed to spend the evening somewhere, laughed out loudly as the Spirit passed, though little kenned the lamplighter that he had any company but Christmas!

And now, without a word of warning from the Ghost, they stood upon a bleak and desert moor, where monstrous masses of rude stone were cast about, as though it were the burial-place of giants; and water spread itself wheresoever it listed, or would have done so, but for the frost that held it prisoner; and nothing grew but moss and furze, and coarse rank grass. Down in the west the setting sun had left a streak of fiery red, which glared upon the desolation for an instant, like a sullen eye, and frowning lower, lower, lower yet, was lost in the thick gloom of darkest night.

"What place is this?" asked Scrooge.

"A place where Miners live, who labour in the bowels of the earth," returned the Spirit. "But they know me. See!"

A light shone from the window of a hut, and swiftly they advanced towards it. Passing through the wall of mud and stone, they found a cheerful company assembled round a glowing fire. An old, old man and woman, with their children and their children's children, and another generation beyond that, all decked out gaily in their holiday attire. The old man, in a voice that

seldom rose above the howling of the wind upon the barren waste, was singing them a Christmas song—it had been a very old song when he was a boy—and from time to time they all joined in the chorus. So surely as they raised their voices, the old man got quite blithe and loud; and so surely as they stopped, his vigour sank again.

The Spirit did not tarry here, but bade Scrooge hold his robe, and passing on above the moor, sped—whither? Not to sea? To sea. To Scrooge's horror, looking back, he saw the last of the land, a frightful range of rocks, behind them; and his ears were deafened by the thundering of water, as it rolled and roared, and raged among the dreadful caverns it had worn, and fiercely tried to undermine the earth.

Built upon a dismal reef of sunken rocks, some league or so from shore, on which the waters chafed and dashed, the wild year through, there stood a solitary lighthouse. Great heaps of sea-weed clung to its base, and storm-birds —born of the wind one might suppose, as sea-weed of the water—rose and fell about it, like the waves they skimmed.

But even here, two men who watched the light had made a fire, that through the loophole in the thick stone wall shed out a ray of brightness on the awful sea. Joining their horny hands over the rough table at which they sat, they wished each other Merry Christmas in their can of grog; and one of them: the elder, too, with his face all damaged and scarred with hard weather, as the figure-head of an old ship might be: struck up a sturdy song that was like a Gale in itself.

Again the Ghost sped on, above the black and heaving sea — on, on—until, being far away, as he told Scrooge, from any shore, they lighted on a ship. They stood beside the helmsman at the wheel, the look-out in the bow, the officers who had the watch; dark, ghostly figures in their several stations; but every man among them hummed a Christmas tune, or had a Christmas thought, or spoke below his breath to his companion of some bygone Christmas Day, with homeward hopes belonging to it. And every man on board, waking or sleeping, good or bad, had had a kinder word for another on that day than on any day in the year; and had shared to some extent in its festivities; and had remembered those he cared for at a distance, and had known that they delighted to remember him.

It was a great surprise to Scrooge, while listening to the moaning of the wind, and thinking what a solemn thing it was to move on through the lonely darkness over an unknown abyss, whose depths were secrets as profound as Death: it was a great surprise to Scrooge, while thus engaged, to hear a hearty laugh. It was a much greater surprise to Scrooge to recognise it as his own nephew's and to find himself in a bright, dry, gleaming room, with the Spirit standing smiling by his side, and looking at that same nephew with approving affability!

"Ha, ha!" laughed Scrooge's nephew. "Ha, ha, ha!"

If you should happen, by any unlikely chance, to know a man more blest in a laugh than Scrooge's nephew, all I can say is, I should like to know him too. Introduce him to me, and I'll cultivate his acquaintance.

It is a fair, even-handed, noble adjustment of things, that while there is infection in disease and sorrow, there is nothing in the world so irresistibly contagious as laughter and good-humour. When Scrooge's nephew laughed in this way: holding his sides, rolling his head, and twisting his face into the most extravagant contortions: Scrooge's niece, by marriage, laughed as heartily as he. And their assembled friends being not a bit behindhand, roared out lustily.

"Ha, ha! Ha, ha, ha, ha!"

"He said that Christmas was a humbug, as I live!" cried Scrooge's nephew. "He believed it too!"

"More shame for him, Fred!" said Scrooge's niece, indignantly. Bless those women; they never do anything by halves. They are always in earnest.

She was very pretty: exceedingly pretty. With a dimpled, surprised-looking, capital face; a ripe little mouth, that seemed made to be kissed—as no doubt it was; all kinds of good little dots about her chin, that melted into one another when she laughed; and the sunniest pair of eyes you ever saw in any little creature's head. Altogether she was what you would have called provoking, you know; but satisfactory, too. Oh, perfectly satisfactory.

"He's a comical old fellow," said Scrooge's nephew, "that's the truth: and not so pleasant as he might be. However, his offences carry their own punishment, and I have nothing to say against him."

"I'm sure he is very rich, Fred," hinted Scrooge's niece. "At least you always tell me so."

"What of that, my dear!" said Scrooge's nephew. "His wealth is of no use to him. He don't do any good with it. He don't make himself comfortable with it. He hasn't the satisfaction of thinking—ha, ha, ha!—that he is ever going to benefit US with it."

"I have no patience with him," observed Scrooge's niece. Scrooge's niece's sisters, and all the other ladies, expressed the same opinion.

"Oh, I have!" said Scrooge's nephew. "I am sorry for him; I couldn't be angry with him if I tried. Who suffers by his ill whims! Himself, always. Here, he takes it into his head to dislike us, and he won't come and dine with us. What's the consequence? He don't lose much of a dinner."

"Indeed, I think he loses a very good dinner," interrupted Scrooge's niece. Everybody else said the same, and they must be allowed to have been competent judges, because they had just had dinner; and, with the dessert upon the table, were clustered round the fire, by lamplight.

"Well! I'm very glad to hear it," said Scrooge's nephew, "because I haven't great faith in these young housekeepers. What do you say, Topper?"

Topper had clearly got his eye upon one of Scrooge's niece's sisters, for he answered that a bachelor was a wretched outcast, who had no right to express an opinion on the subject. Whereat Scrooge's niece's sister—the plump one with the lace tucker: not the one with the roses—blushed.

"Do go on, Fred," said Scrooge's niece, clapping her hands. "He never finishes what he begins to say! He is such a ridiculous fellow!"

Scrooge's nephew revelled in another laugh, and as it was impossible to keep the infection off; though the plump sister tried hard to do it with aromatic vinegar; his example was unanimously followed.

"I was only going to say," said Scrooge's nephew, "that the consequence of his taking a dislike to us, and not making merry with us, is, as I think, that he loses some pleasant moments, which could do him no harm. I am sure he loses pleasanter companions than he can find in his own thoughts, either in his mouldy old office, or his dusty chambers. I mean to give him the same chance every year, whether he likes it or not, for I pity him. He may rail at Christmas till he dies, but he can't help thinking better of it—I defy him—if he finds me going there, in good temper, year after year, and saying Uncle Scrooge, how are you? If it only puts him in the vein to leave his poor clerk fifty pounds, that's something; and I think I shook him yesterday."

It was their turn to laugh now at the notion of his shaking

Scrooge. But being thoroughly good-natured, and not much caring what they laughed at, so that they laughed at any rate, he encouraged them in their merriment, and passed the bottle joyously.

After tea, they had some music. For they were a musical family, and knew what they were about, when they sung a Glee or Catch, I can assure you: especially Topper, who could growl away in the bass like a good one, and never swell the large veins in his forehead, or get red in the face over it. Scrooge's niece played well upon the harp; and played among other tunes a simple little air (a mere nothing: you might learn to whistle it in two minutes), which

had been familiar to the child who fetched Scrooge from the boarding-school, as he had been reminded by the Ghost of Christmas Past. When this strain of music sounded, all the things that Ghost had shown him, came upon his mind; he softened more and more; and thought that if he could have listened to it often, years ago, he might have cultivated the kindnesses of life for his own happiness with his own hands, without resorting to the sexton's spade that buried Jacob Marley.

But they didn't devote the whole evening to music. After a while they played at forfeits; for it is good to be children sometimes, and never better than at Christmas, when its mighty Founder was a child himself. Stop! There was first a game at blind-man's buff. Of course there was. And I no more believe Topper was really blind than I believe he had eyes in his boots. My opinion is, that it was a done thing between him and Scrooge's nephew; and that the Ghost of Christmas Present knew it. The way he went after that plump sister in the lace tucker, was an outrage on the credulity of human nature. Knocking down the fire-irons, tumbling over the chairs, bumping against the piano, smothering himself among the curtains, wherever she went, there went he! He always knew where the plump sister was. He wouldn't catch anybody else. If you had fallen up against him (as some of them did), on purpose, he would have made a feint of endeavouring to seize you, which would have been an affront to your understanding, and would instantly have sidled off in the direction of the plump sister. She often cried out that it wasn't fair; and it really was not. But when at last, he caught her; when, in spite of all her silken rustlings, and her rapid flutterings past him, he got her into a corner whence there was no escape; then his conduct was the most execrable. For his pretending not to know her; his pretending that it was necessary to touch her head-dress, and further to assure himself of her identity by pressing a certain ring upon her finger, and a certain chain about her neck; was vile, monstrous! No doubt she told him her opinion of it, when, another blind-man being in office, they were so very confidential together, behind the curtains.

Scrooge's niece was not one of the blind-man's buff party, but was made comfortable with a large chair and a footstool, in a snug corner, where the Ghost and Scrooge were close behind her. But she joined in the forfeits, and loved her love to admiration with all the letters of the alphabet. Likewise at the game of How, When, and Where, she was very great, and to the secret joy of Scrooge's nephew, beat her sisters hollow: though they were sharp girls too, as Topper could have told you. There might have been twenty people there, young and old, but they all played, and so did Scrooge; for wholly forgetting in the interest he had in what was going on, that his voice made no sound in their ears, he sometimes came out with his guess quite loud, and very often guessed quite right, too; for the sharpest needle, best Whitechapel, warranted not to cut in the eye, was not sharper than Scrooge; blunt as he took it in his head to be.

The Ghost was greatly pleased to find him in this mood, and looked upon him with such favour, that he begged like a boy to be allowed to stay until the guests departed. But this the Spirit said could not be done.

"Here is a new game," said Scrooge. "One half hour, Spirit, only one!"

It was a Game called Yes and No, where Scrooge's nephew had to think of something, and the rest must find out what; he only answering to their questions yes or no, as the case was. The brisk fire of questioning to which he was exposed, elicited from him that he was thinking of an animal, a live animal, rather a disagreeable animal, a savage animal, an animal that growled and grunted sometimes, and talked sometimes, and lived in London, and walked about the streets, and wasn't made a show of, and wasn't led by anybody, and didn't live in a menagerie, and was never killed in a market, and was not a horse, or an ass, or a cow, or a bull, or a tiger, or a dog, or a pig, or a cat, or a bear. At every fresh question that was put to him, this nephew burst into a fresh roar of laughter; and was so inexpressibly tickled, that he was obliged to get up off the sofa and stamp. At last the plump sister, falling into a similar state, cried out:

"I have found it out! I know what it is, Fred! I know what it is!"

"What is it?" cried Fred.

"It's your Uncle Scro-o-o-o-oge!"

Which it certainly was. Admiration was the universal sentiment, though some objected that the reply to "Is it a bear?" ought to have been "Yes;" inasmuch as an answer in the negative was sufficient to have diverted their thoughts from Mr. Scrooge, supposing they had ever had any tendency that way.

"He has given us plenty of merriment, I am sure," said Fred, "and it would be ungrateful not to drink his health. Here is a glass of mulled wine ready to our hand at the moment; and I say, 'Uncle Scrooge!'"

"Well! Uncle Scrooge!" they cried.

"A Merry Christmas and a Happy New Year to the old man, whatever he is!" said Scrooge's nephew. "He wouldn't take it from me, but may he have it, nevertheless. Uncle Scrooge!"

Uncle Scrooge had imperceptibly become so gay and light of heart, that he would have pledged the unconscious company in return, and thanked them in an inaudible speech, if the Ghost had given him time. But the whole scene passed off in the breath of the last word spoken by his nephew; and he and the Spirit were again upon their travels.

Much they saw, and far they went, and many homes they visited, but always with a happy end. The Spirit stood beside sick beds, and they were cheerful; on foreign lands, and they were close at home; by struggling men, and they were patient in their greater hope; by poverty, and it was rich. In almshouse, hospital, and jail,

in misery's every refuge, where vain man in his little brief authority had not made fast the door, and barred the Spirit out, he left his blessing, and taught Scrooge his precepts.

It was a long night, if it were only a night; but Scrooge had his doubts of this, because the Christmas Holidays appeared to be condensed into the space of time they passed together. It was strange, too, that while Scrooge remained unaltered in his outward form, the Ghost grew older, clearly older. Scrooge had observed this change, but never spoke of it, until they left a children's Twelfth Night party, when, looking at the Spirit as they stood together in an open place, he noticed that its hair was grey.

"Are spirits' lives so short?" asked Scrooge.

"My life upon this globe, is very brief," replied the Ghost. "It ends to-night."

"To-night!" cried Scrooge.

"To-night at midnight. Hark! The time is drawing near."

The chimes were ringing the three quarters past eleven at that moment.

"Forgive me if I am not justified in what I ask," said Scrooge, looking intently at the Spirit's robe, "but I see something strange, and not belonging to yourself, protruding from your skirts. Is it a foot or a claw?"

"It might be a claw, for the flesh there is upon it," was the Spirit's sorrowful reply. "Look here."

From the foldings of its robe, it brought two children;

wretched, abject, frightful, hideous, miserable. They knelt down at its feet, and clung upon the outside of its garment.

"Oh, Man! look here. Look, look, down here!" exclaimed the Ghost.

They were a boy and girl. Yellow, meagre, ragged, scowling, wolfish; but prostrate, too, in their humility. Where graceful youth should have filled their features out, and touched them with its freshest tints, a stale and shrivelled hand, like that of age, had pinched, and twisted them, and pulled them into shreds. Where angels might have sat enthroned, devils lurked, and glared out menacing. No change, no degradation, no perversion of humanity, in any grade, through all the mysteries of wonderful creation, has monsters half so horrible and dread.

Scrooge started back, appalled. Having them shown to him in this way, he tried to say they were fine children, but the words choked themselves, rather than be parties to a lie of such enormous magnitude.

"Spirit! are they yours?" Scrooge could say no more.

"They are Man's," said the Spirit, looking down upon them. "And they cling to me, appealing from their fathers. This boy is Ignorance. This girl is Want. Beware them both, and all of their degree, but most of all beware this boy, for on his brow I see that written which is Doom, unless the writing be erased. Deny it!" cried the Spirit, stretching out its hand towards the city. "Slander those who tell it ye! Admit it for your factious purposes, and make it worse. And bide the end!"

"Have they no refuge or resource?" cried Scrooge.

"Are there no prisons?" said the Spirit, turning on him for the last time with his own words. "Are there no workhouses?"

The bell struck twelve.

Scrooge looked about him for the Ghost, and saw it not. As the last stroke ceased to vibrate, he remembered the prediction of old Jacob Marley, and lifting up his eyes,

beheld a solemn Phantom, draped and hooded, coming, like a mist along the ground, towards him.

STAVE IV

THE LAST OF THE SPIRITS

THE Phantom slowly, gravely, silently, approached. When it came near him, Scrooge bent down upon his knee; for in the very air through which this Spirit moved it seemed to scatter gloom and mystery.

It was shrouded in a deep black garment, which concealed its head, its face, its form, and left nothing of it visible save one outstretched hand. But for this it would have been difficult to detach its figure from the night, and separate it from the darkness by which it was surrounded.

He felt that it was tall and stately when it came beside him, and that its mysterious presence filled him with a solemn dread. He knew no more, for the Spirit neither spoke nor moved.

"I am in the presence of the Ghost of Christmas Yet To Come?" said Scrooge.

The Spirit answered not, but pointed onward with its hand.

"You are about to show me shadows of the things that have not happened, but will happen in the time before us," Scrooge pursued. "Is that so, Spirit?"

The upper portion of the garment was contracted for an

instant in its folds, as if the Spirit had inclined its head. That was the only answer he received.

Although well used to ghostly company by this time, Scrooge feared the silent shape so much that his legs trembled beneath him, and he found that he could hardly stand when he prepared to follow it. The Spirit paused a moment, as observing his condition, and giving him time to recover.

But Scrooge was all the worse for this. It thrilled him with a vague uncertain horror, to know that behind the dusky shroud, there were ghostly eyes intently fixed upon him, while he, though he stretched his own to the utmost, could see nothing but a spectral hand and one great heap of black.

"Ghost of the Future!" he exclaimed, "I fear you more than any spectre I have seen. But as I know your purpose is to do me good, and as I hope to live to be another man from what I was, I am prepared to bear you company, and do it with a thankful heart. Will you not speak to me?"

It gave him no reply. The hand was pointed straight before them.

"Lead on!" said Scrooge. "Lead on! The night is waning fast, and it is precious time to me, I know. Lead on, Spirit!"

The Phantom moved away as it had come towards him. Scrooge followed in the shadow of its dress, which bore him up, he thought, and carried him along.

They scarcely seemed to enter the city; for the city rather

seemed to spring up about them, and encompass them of its own act. But there they were, in the heart of it; on 'Change, amongst the merchants; who hurried up and down, and chinked the money in their pockets, and conversed in groups, and looked at their watches, and trifled thoughtfully with their great gold seals; and so forth, as Scrooge had seen them often.

The Spirit stopped beside one little knot of business men. Observing that the hand was pointed to them, Scrooge advanced to listen to their talk.

"No," said a great fat man with a monstrous chin, "I don't know much about it, either way. I only know he's dead."

"When did he die?" inquired another.

"Last night, I believe."

"Why, what was the matter with him?" asked a third, taking a vast quantity of snuff out of a very large snuff-box. "I thought he'd never die."

"God knows," said the first, with a yawn.

"What has he done with his money?" asked a red-faced gentleman with a pendulous excrescence on the end of his nose, that shook like the gills of a turkey-cock.

"I haven't heard," said the man with the large chin, yawning again. "Left it to his company, perhaps. He hasn't left it to me. That's all I know."

This pleasantry was received with a general laugh.

"It's likely to be a very cheap funeral," said the same speaker;

"for upon my life I don't know of anybody to go to it. Suppose we make up a party and volunteer?"

"I don't mind going if a lunch is provided," observed the gentleman with the excrescence on his nose. "But I must be fed, if I make one."

Another laugh.

"Well, I am the most disinterested among you, after all," said the first speaker, "for I never wear black gloves, and I never eat lunch. But I'll offer to go, if anybody else will. When I come to think of it, I'm not at all sure that I wasn't his most particular friend; for we used to stop and speak whenever we met. Bye, bye!"

Speakers and listeners strolled away, and mixed with other groups. Scrooge knew the men, and looked towards the Spirit for an explanation.

The Phantom glided on into a street. Its finger pointed to two persons meeting. Scrooge listened again, thinking that the explanation might lie here.

He knew these men, also, perfectly. They were men of business: very wealthy, and of great importance. He had made a point always of standing well in their esteem: in a business point of view, that is; strictly in a business point of view.

"How are you?" said one.

"How are you?" returned the other.

"Well!" said the first. "Old Scratch has got his own at last, hey?"

"So I am told," returned the second. "Cold, isn't it?"

"Seasonable for Christmas time. You're not a skater, I suppose?"

"No. No. Something else to think of. Good morning!"

Not another word. That was their meeting, their conversation, and their parting.

Scrooge was at first inclined to be surprised that the Spirit should attach importance to conversations apparently so trivial; but feeling assured that they must have some hidden purpose, he set himself to consider what it was likely to be. They could scarcely be supposed to have any bearing on the death of Jacob, his old partner, for that was Past, and this Ghost's province was the Future. Nor could he think of any one immediately connected with himself, to whom he could apply them. But nothing doubting that to whomsoever they applied they had some latent moral for his own improvement, he resolved to treasure up every word he heard, and everything he saw; and especially to observe the shadow of himself when it appeared. For he had an expectation that the conduct of his future self would give him the clue he missed, and would render the solution of these riddles easy.

He looked about in that very place for his own image; but another man stood in his accustomed corner, and though the clock pointed to his usual time of day for being there, he saw no likeness of himself among the multitudes that poured in through the Porch. It gave him little surprise, however; for he had been revolving in his mind a change of life, and thought and hoped he saw his new-born resolutions carried out in this.

Quiet and dark, beside him stood the Phantom, with its outstretched hand. When he roused himself from his thoughtful quest, he fancied from the turn of the hand, and its situation in reference to himself, that the Unseen Eyes were looking at him keenly. It made him shudder, and feel very cold.

They left the busy scene, and went into an obscure part of the town, where Scrooge had never penetrated before, although he recognised its situation, and its bad repute. The ways were foul and narrow; the shops and houses wretched; the people half-naked, drunken, slipshod, ugly. Alleys and archways, like so many cesspools, disgorged their offences of smell, and dirt, and life, upon the straggling streets; and the whole quarter reeked with crime, with filth, and misery.

Far in this den of infamous resort, there was a low-browed, beetling shop, below a pent-house roof, where iron, old rags, bottles, bones, and greasy offal, were bought. Upon the floor within, were piled up heaps of rusty keys, nails, chains, hinges, files, scales, weights, and refuse iron of all kinds. Secrets that few would like to scrutinise were bred and hidden in mountains of unseemly rags, masses of corrupted fat, and sepulchres of bones. Sitting in among the wares he dealt in, by a charcoal stove, made of old bricks, was a grey-haired rascal, nearly seventy years of age; who had screened himself from the cold air without, by a frousy

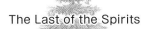

curtaining of miscellaneous tatters, hung upon a line; and smoked his pipe in all the luxury of calm retirement.

Scrooge and the Phantom came into the presence of this man, just as a woman with a heavy bundle slunk into the shop. But she had scarcely entered, when another woman, similarly laden, came in too; and she was closely followed by a man in faded black, who was no less startled by the sight of them, than they had been upon the recognition of each other. After a short period of blank astonishment, in which the old man with the pipe had joined them, they all three burst into a laugh.

"Let the charwoman alone to be the first!" cried she who had entered first. "Let the laundress alone to be the second; and let the undertaker's man alone to be the third. Look here, old Joe, here's a chance! If we haven't all three met here without meaning it!"

"You couldn't have met in a better place," said old Joe, removing his pipe from his mouth. "Come into the parlour. You were made free of it long ago, you know; and the other two an't strangers. Stop till I shut the door of the shop. Ah! How it skreeks! There an't such a rusty bit of metal in the place as its own hinges, I believe; and I'm sure there's no such old bones here, as mine. Ha, ha! We're all suitable to our calling, we're well matched. Come into the parlour. Come into the parlour."

The parlour was the space behind the screen of rags. The old man raked the fire together with an old stair-rod, and having trimmed his smoky lamp (for it was night), with the stem of his pipe, put it in his mouth again.

While he did this, the woman who had already spoken threw her bundle on the floor, and sat down in a flaunting manner on a stool; crossing her elbows on her knees, and looking with a bold defiance at the other two.

"What odds then! What odds, Mrs. Dilber?" said the woman. "Every person has a right to take care of themselves. He always did."

"That's true, indeed!" said the laundress. "No man more so."

"Why then, don't stand staring as if you was afraid, woman;

who's the wiser? We're not going to pick holes in each other's coats, I suppose?"

"No, indeed!" said Mrs. Dilber and the man together. "We should hope not."

"Very well, then!" cried the woman. "That's enough. Who's the worse for the loss of a few things like these? Not a dead man, I suppose."

"No, indeed," said Mrs. Dilber, laughing.

"If he wanted to keep 'em after he was dead, a wicked old screw," pursued the woman, "why wasn't he natural in his lifetime? If he had been, he'd have had somebody to look after him when he was struck with Death, instead of lying gasping out his last there, alone by himself."

"It's the truest word that ever was spoke," said Mrs. Dilber. "It's a judgment on him."

"I wish it was a little heavier judgment," replied the woman; "and it should have been, you may depend upon it, if I could have laid my hands on anything else. Open that bundle, old Joe, and let me know the value of it. Speak out plain. I'm not afraid to be the first, nor afraid for them to see it. We know pretty well that we were helping ourselves, before we met here, I believe. It's no sin. Open the bundle, Joe."

But the gallantry of her friends would not allow of this; and the man in faded black, mounting the breach first, produced his plunder. It was not extensive. A seal or two, a pencil-case, a pair of sleeve-buttons, and a brooch of no great value, were all. They were severally examined and appraised by old Joe, who chalked the sums he was disposed to give for each, upon the wall, and added them up into a total when he found there was nothing more to come.

"That's your account," said Joe, "and I wouldn't give another sixpence, if I was to be boiled for not doing it. Who's next?"

Mrs. Dilber was next. Sheets and towels, a little wearing apparel, two old-fashioned silver teaspoons, a pair of sugar-tongs, and a few boots. Her account was stated on the wall in the same manner.

"I always give too much to ladies. It's a weakness of mine, and that's the way I ruin myself," said old Joe. "That's your account. If you asked me for another penny, and made it an open question, I'd repent of being so liberal and knock off half-a-crown."

"And now undo my bundle, Joe," said the first woman.

Joe went down on his knees for the greater convenience of opening it, and having unfastened a great many knots, dragged out a large and heavy roll of some dark stuff.

"What do you call this?" said Joe. "Bed-curtains!"

"Ah!" returned the woman, laughing and leaning forward on her crossed arms. "Bed-curtains!"

"You don't mean to say you took 'em down, rings and all, with him lying there?" said Joe.

"Yes I do," replied the woman. "Why not?"

"You were born to make your fortune," said Joe, "and you'll certainly do it."

"I certainly shan't hold my hand, when I can get anything in it by reaching it out, for the sake of such a man as He was, I promise you, Joe," returned the woman coolly. "Don't drop that oil upon the blankets, now."

"His blankets?" asked Joe.

"Whose else's do you think?" replied the woman. "He isn't likely to take cold without 'em, I dare say."

"I hope he didn't die of anything catching? Eh?" said old Joe, stopping in his work, and looking up.

"Don't you be afraid of that," returned the woman. "I an't so fond of his company that I'd loiter about him for such things, if he did. Ah! you may look through that shirt till your eyes ache; but you won't find a hole in it, nor a threadbare place. It's the best he had, and a fine one too. They'd have wasted it, if it hadn't been for me."

"What do you call wasting of it?" asked old Joe.

"Putting it on him to be buried in, to be sure," replied the woman with a laugh. "Somebody was fool enough to do it, but I took it off again. If calico an't good enough for such a purpose, it isn't good enough for anything. It's quite as becoming to the body. He can't look uglier than he did in that one."

Scrooge listened to this dialogue in horror. As they sat

grouped about their spoil, in the scanty light afforded by the old man's lamp, he viewed them with a detestation and disgust, which could hardly have been greater, though they had been obscene demons, marketing the corpse itself.

"Ha, ha!" laughed the same woman, when old Joe, producing a flannel bag with money in it, told out their several gains upon the ground. "This is the end of it, you see! He frightened every one away from him when he was alive, to profit us when he was dead! Ha, ha, ha!"

"Spirit!" said Scrooge, shuddering from head to foot. "I see, I see. The case of this unhappy man might be my own. My life tends that way, now. Merciful Heaven, what is this!"

He recoiled in terror, for the scene had changed, and now he almost touched a bed: a bare, uncurtained bed: on which, beneath a ragged sheet, there lay a something covered up, which, though it was dumb, announced itself in awful language.

The room was very dark, too dark to be observed with any accuracy, though Scrooge glanced round it in obedience to a secret impulse, anxious to know what kind of room it was. A pale light, rising in the outer air, fell straight upon the bed; and on it, plundered and bereft, unwatched, unwept, uncared for, was the body of this man.

Scrooge glanced towards the Phantom. Its steady hand was pointed to the head. The cover was so carelessly adjusted that the slightest raising of it, the motion of a finger upon Scrooge's part,

would have disclosed the face. He thought of it, felt how easy it would be to do, and longed to do it; but had no more power to withdraw the veil than to dismiss the spectre at his side.

Oh cold, cold, rigid, dreadful Death, set up thine altar here, and dress it with such terrors as thou hast at thy command: for this is thy dominion! But of the loved, revered, and honoured head, thou canst not turn one hair to thy dread purposes, or make one feature odious. It is not that the hand is heavy and will fall down when released; it is not that the heart and pulse are still; but that the hand WAS open, generous, and true; the heart brave, warm, and tender; and the pulse a man's. Strike, Shadow, strike! And see his good deeds springing from the wound, to sow the world with life immortal!

No voice pronounced these words in Scrooge's ears, and yet he heard them when he looked upon the bed. He thought, if this man could be raised up now, what would be his foremost thoughts? Avarice, hard-dealing, griping cares? They have brought him to a rich end, truly!

He lay, in the dark empty house, with not a man, a woman, or a child, to say that he was kind to me in this or that, and for the memory of one kind word I will be kind to him. A cat was tearing at the door, and there was a sound of gnawing rats beneath the hearth-stone. What they wanted in the room of death, and why they were so restless and disturbed, Scrooge did not dare to think.

"Spirit!" he said, "this is a fearful place. In leaving it, I shall not leave its lesson, trust me. Let us go!"

Still the Ghost pointed with an unmoved finger to the head.

"I understand you," Scrooge returned, "and I would do it, if I could. But I have not the power, Spirit. I have not the power."

Again it seemed to look upon him.

"If there is any person in the town, who feels emotion caused by this man's death," said Scrooge quite agonised, "show that person to me, Spirit, I beseech you!"

The Phantom spread its dark robe before him for a moment, like a wing; and withdrawing it, revealed a room by daylight, where a mother and her children were.

She was expecting some one, and with anxious eagerness; for she walked up and down the room; started at every sound; looked out from the window; glanced at the clock; tried, but in vain, to work with her needle; and could hardly bear the voices of the children in their play.

At length the long-expected knock was heard. She hurried to the door, and met her husband; a man whose face was careworn and depressed, though he was young. There was a remarkable expression in it now; a kind of serious delight of which he felt ashamed, and which he struggled to repress.

He sat down to the dinner that had been hoarding for him by the fire; and when she asked him faintly what news (which was not until after a long silence), he appeared embarrassed how to answer.

"Is it good?" she said, "or bad?"—to help him.

"Bad," he answered.

"We are quite ruined?"

"No. There is hope yet, Caroline."

"If he relents," she said, amazed, "there is! Nothing is past hope, if such a miracle has happened."

"He is past relenting," said her husband. "He is dead."

She was a mild and patient creature if her face spoke truth; but she was thankful in her soul to hear it, and she said so, with clasped hands. She prayed forgiveness the next moment, and was sorry; but the first was the emotion of her heart.

"What the half-drunken woman whom I told you of last night, said to me, when I tried to see him and obtain a week's delay; and what I thought was a mere excuse to avoid me; turns out to have been quite true. He was not only very ill, but dying, then."

"To whom will our debt be transferred?"

"I don't know. But before that time we shall be ready with the money; and even though we were not, it would be a bad fortune indeed to find so merciless a creditor in his successor. We may sleep to-night with light hearts, Caroline!"

Yes. Soften it as they would, their hearts were lighter. The children's faces, hushed and clustered round to hear what they so little understood, were brighter; and it was a happier house for this man's death! The only emotion that the Ghost could show him,

243

caused by the event, was one of pleasure.

"Let me see some tenderness connected with a death," said Scrooge; "or that dark chamber, Spirit, which we left just now, will be for ever present to me."

The Ghost conducted him through several streets familiar to his feet; and as they went along, Scrooge looked here and there to find himself, but nowhere was he to be seen. They entered poor Bob Cratchit's house; the dwelling he had visited before; and found the mother and the children seated round the fire.

Quiet. Very quiet. The noisy little Cratchits were as still as statues in one corner, and sat looking up at Peter, who had a book before him. The mother and her daughters were engaged in sewing. But surely they were very quiet!

"'And He took a child, and set him in the midst of them.'"

Where had Scrooge heard those words? He had not dreamed them. The boy must have read them out, as he and the Spirit crossed the threshold. Why did he not go on?

The mother laid her work upon the table, and put her hand up to her face.

"The colour hurts my eyes," she said.

The colour? Ah, poor Tiny Tim!

"They're better now again," said Cratchit's wife. "It makes them weak by candle-light; and I wouldn't show weak eyes to your father when he comes home, for the world. It must be near his time."

"Past it rather," Peter answered, shutting up his book.

"But I think he has walked a little slower than he used, these few last evenings, mother."

They were very quiet again. At last she said, and in a steady, cheerful voice, that only faltered once:

"I have known him walk with—I have known him walk with Tiny Tim upon his shoulder, very fast indeed."

"And so have I," cried Peter. "Often."

"And so have I," exclaimed another. So had all.

"But he was very light to carry," she resumed, intent upon her work, "and his father loved him so, that it was no trouble: no trouble. And there is your father at the door!"

She hurried out to meet him; and little Bob in his comforter —he had need of it, poor fellow—came in. His tea was ready for him on the hob, and they all tried who should help him to it most. Then the two young Cratchits got upon his knees and laid, each child a little cheek, against his face, as if they said, "Don't mind it, father. Don't be grieved!"

Bob was very cheerful with them, and spoke pleasantly to all the family. He looked at the work upon the table, and praised the industry and speed of Mrs. Cratchit and the girls. They would be done long before Sunday, he said.

"Sunday! You went to-day, then, Robert?" said his wife.

"Yes, my dear," returned Bob. "I wish you could have gone. It would have done you good to see how green a place it is. But

you'll see it often. I promised him that I would walk there on a Sunday. My little, little child!" cried Bob. "My little child!"

He broke down all at once. He couldn't help it. If he could have helped it, he and his child would have been farther apart perhaps than they were.

He left the room, and went up-stairs into the room above, which was lighted cheerfully, and hung with Christmas. There was a chair set close beside the child, and there were signs of some one having been there, lately. Poor Bob sat down in it, and when he had thought a little and composed himself, he kissed the little

face. He was reconciled to what had happened, and went down again quite happy.

They drew about the fire, and talked; the girls and mother working still. Bob told them of the extraordinary kindness of Mr. Scrooge's nephew, whom he had scarcely seen but once, and who, meeting him in the street that day, and seeing that he looked a little—"just a little down you know," said Bob, inquired what had happened to distress him. "On which," said Bob, "for he is the pleasantest-spoken gentleman you ever heard, I told him. 'I am heartily sorry for it, Mr. Cratchit,' he said, 'and heartily sorry for your good wife.' By the bye, how he ever knew that, I don't know."

"Knew what, my dear?"

"Why, that you were a good wife," replied Bob.

"Everybody knows that!" said Peter.

"Very well observed, my boy!" cried Bob. "I hope they do. 'Heartily sorry,' he said, 'for your good wife. If I can be of service to you in any way,' he said, giving me his card, 'that's where I live. Pray come to me.' Now, it wasn't," cried Bob, "for the sake of anything he might be able to do for us, so much as for his kind way, that this was quite delightful. It really seemed as if he had known our Tiny Tim, and felt with us."

"I'm sure he's a good soul!" said Mrs. Cratchit.

"You would be surer of it, my dear," returned Bob, "if you saw and spoke to him. I shouldn't be at all surprised— mark what I say!—if he got Peter a better situation."

"Only hear that, Peter," said Mrs. Cratchit.

"And then," cried one of the girls, "Peter will be keeping company with some one, and setting up for himself."

"Get along with you!" retorted Peter, grinning.

"It's just as likely as not," said Bob, "one of these days; though there's plenty of time for that, my dear. But however and whenever we part from one another, I am sure we shall none of us forget poor Tiny Tim—shall we—or this first parting that there was among us?"

"Never, father!" cried they all.

"And I know," said Bob, "I know, my dears, that when we recollect how patient and how mild he was; although he was a little, little child; we shall not quarrel easily among ourselves, and forget poor Tiny Tim in doing it."

"No, never, father!" they all cried again.

"I am very happy," said little Bob, "I am very happy!"

Mrs. Cratchit kissed him, his daughters kissed him, the two young Cratchits kissed him, and Peter and himself shook hands. Spirit of Tiny Tim, thy childish essence was from God!

"Spectre," said Scrooge, "something informs me that our parting moment is at hand. I know it, but I know not how. Tell me what man that was whom we saw lying dead?"

The Ghost of Christmas Yet To Come conveyed him, as before—though at a different time, he thought: indeed, there seemed no order in these latter visions, save that they were in the

Future—into the resorts of business men, but showed him not himself. Indeed, the Spirit did not stay for anything, but went straight on, as to the end just now desired, until besought by Scrooge to tarry for a moment.

"This court," said Scrooge, "through which we hurry now, is where my place of occupation is, and has been for a length of time. I see the house. Let me behold what I shall be, in days to come!"

The Spirit stopped; the hand was pointed elsewhere.

"The house is yonder," Scrooge exclaimed. "Why do you point away?"

The inexorable finger underwent no change.

Scrooge hastened to the window of his office, and looked in. It was an office still, but not his. The furniture was not the same, and the figure in the chair was not himself. The Phantom pointed as before.

He joined it once again, and wondering why and whither he had gone, accompanied it until they reached an iron gate. He paused to look round before entering.

A churchyard. Here, then; the wretched man whose name he had now to learn, lay underneath the ground. It was a worthy place. Walled in by houses; overrun by grass and weeds, the growth of vegetation's death, not life; choked up with too much burying; fat with repleted appetite. A worthy place!

The Spirit stood among the graves, and pointed down to One. He advanced towards it trembling. The Phantom was exactly

as it had been, but he dreaded that he saw new meaning in its solemn shape.

"Before I draw nearer to that stone to which you point," said Scrooge, "answer me one question. Are these the shadows of the things that Will be, or are they shadows of things that May be, only?"

Still the Ghost pointed downward to the grave by which it stood.

"Men's courses will foreshadow certain ends, to which, if persevered in, they must lead," said Scrooge. "But if the courses be departed from, the ends will change. Say it is thus with what you show me!"

The Spirit was immovable as ever.

Scrooge crept towards it, trembling as he went; and following the finger, read upon the stone of the neglected grave his own name, EBENEZER SCROOGE.

"Am I that man who lay upon the bed?" he cried, upon his knees.

The finger pointed from the grave to him, and back again.

"No, Spirit! Oh no, no!"

The finger still was there.

"Spirit!" he cried, tight clutching at its robe, "hear me! I am not the man I was. I will not be the man I must have been but for this intercourse. Why show me this, if I am past all hope!"

For the first time the hand appeared to shake.

"Good Spirit," he pursued, as down upon the ground he fell before it: "Your nature intercedes for me, and pities me. Assure me that I yet may change these shadows you have shown me, by an altered life!"

The kind hand trembled.

"I will honour Christmas in my heart, and try to keep it all the year. I will live in the Past, the Present, and the Future. The Spirits of all Three shall strive within me. I will not shut out the lessons that they teach. Oh, tell me I may sponge away the writing on this stone!"

In his agony, he caught the spectral hand. It sought to free itself, but he was strong in his entreaty, and detained it. The Spirit, stronger yet, repulsed him.

Holding up his hands in a last prayer to have his fate reversed, he saw an alteration in the Phantom's hood and dress. It shrunk, collapsed, and dwindled down into a bedpost.

THE END OF IT

YES! and the bedpost was his own. The bed was his own, the room was his own. Best and happiest of all, the Time before him was his own, to make amends in!

"I will live in the Past, the Present, and the Future!" Scrooge repeated, as he scrambled out of bed. "The Spirits of all Three shall strive within me. Oh Jacob Marley! Heaven, and the Christmas Time be praised for this! I say it on my knees, old Jacob; on my knees!"

He was so fluttered and so glowing with his good intentions, that his broken voice would scarcely answer to his call. He had been sobbing violently in his conflict with the Spirit, and his face was wet with tears.

"They are not torn down," cried Scrooge, folding one of his bed-curtains in his arms, "they are not torn down, rings and all. They are here—I am here—the shadows of the things that would have been, may be dispelled. They will be. I know they will!"

His hands were busy with his garments all this time; turning them inside out, putting them on upside down, tearing them, mislaying them, making them parties to every kind of extravagance.

"I don't know what to do!" cried Scrooge, laughing and crying in the same breath; and making a perfect Laocoön of himself with his stockings. "I am as light as a feather, I am as happy as an angel, I am as merry as a schoolboy. I am as giddy as a drunken man. A merry Christmas to everybody! A happy New Year to all the world. Hallo here! Whoop! Hallo!"

He had frisked into the sitting-room, and was now standing there: perfectly winded.

"There's the saucepan that the gruel was in!" cried Scrooge, starting off again, and going round the fireplace. "There's the door, by which the Ghost of Jacob Marley entered! There's the corner where the Ghost of Christmas Present, sat! There's the window where I saw the wandering Spirits! It's all right, it's all true, it all happened. Ha ha ha!"

Really, for a man who had been out of practice for so many years, it was a splendid laugh, a most illustrious laugh. The father of a long, long line of brilliant laughs!

"I don't know what day of the month it is!" said Scrooge. "I don't know how long I've been among the Spirits. I don't know anything. I'm quite a baby. Never mind. I don't care. I'd rather be a baby. Hallo! Whoop! Hallo here!"

He was checked in his transports by the churches ringing out the lustiest peals he had ever heard. Clash, clang, hammer; ding, dong, bell. Bell, dong, ding; hammer, clang, clash! Oh, glorious, glorious!

The End of It

Running to the window, he opened it, and put out his head. No fog, no mist; clear, bright, jovial, stirring, cold; cold, piping for the blood to dance to; Golden sunlight; Heavenly sky; sweet fresh air; merry bells. Oh, glorious! Glorious!

"What's to-day!" cried Scrooge, calling downward to a boy in Sunday clothes, who perhaps had loitered in to look about him.

"EH?" returned the boy, with all his might of wonder.

"What's to-day, my fine fellow?" said Scrooge.

"To-day!" replied the boy. "Why, CHRISTMAS DAY."

"It's Christmas Day!" said Scrooge to himself. "I haven't missed it. The Spirits have done it all in one night. They can do anything they like. Of course they can. Of course they can. Hallo, my fine fellow!"

"Hallo!" returned the boy.

"Do you know the Poulterer's, in the next street but one, at the corner?" Scrooge inquired.

"I should hope I did," replied the lad.

"An intelligent boy!" said Scrooge. "A remarkable boy! Do you know whether they've sold the prize Turkey that was hanging up there?—Not the little prize Turkey: the big one?"

"What, the one as big as me?" returned the boy.

"What a delightful boy!" said Scrooge. "It's a pleasure to talk to him. Yes, my buck!"

"It's hanging there now," replied the boy.

"Is it?" said Scrooge. "Go and buy it."

"Walk-ER!" exclaimed the boy.

"No, no," said Scrooge, "I am in earnest. Go and buy it, and tell 'em to bring it here, that I may give them the direction where to take it. Come back with the man, and I'll give you a shilling. Come back with him in less than five minutes and I'll give you half-a-crown!"

The boy was off like a shot. He must have had a steady hand at a trigger who could have got a shot off half so fast.

"I'll send it to Bob Cratchit's!" whispered Scrooge, rubbing his hands, and splitting with a laugh. "He sha'n't know who sends it. It's twice the size of Tiny Tim. Joe Miller never made such a joke as sending it to Bob's will be!"

The hand in which he wrote the address was not a steady one, but write it he did, somehow, and went down-stairs to open the street door, ready for the coming of the poulterer's man. As he stood there, waiting his arrival, the knocker caught his eye.

"I shall love it, as long as I live!" cried Scrooge, patting it with his hand. "I scarcely ever looked at it before. What an honest expression it has in its face! It's a wonderful knocker!—Here's the Turkey! Hallo! Whoop! How are you! Merry Christmas!"

It was a Turkey! He never could have stood upon his legs, that bird. He would have snapped 'em short off in a minute, like sticks of sealing-wax.

"Why, it's impossible to carry that to Camden Town," said Scrooge. "You must have a cab."

The chuckle with which he said this, and the chuckle with which he paid for the Turkey, and the chuckle with which he paid for the cab, and the chuckle with which he recompensed the boy, were only to be exceeded by the chuckle with which he sat down breathless in his chair again, and chuckled till he cried.

Shaving was not an easy task, for his hand continued to shake very much; and shaving requires attention, even when you don't dance while you are at it. But if he had cut the end of his nose off, he would have put a piece of sticking-plaister over it, and been quite satisfied.

He dressed himself "all in his best," and at last got out into the streets. The people were by this time pouring forth, as he had seen them with the Ghost of Christmas Present; and walking with his hands behind him, Scrooge regarded every one with a delighted smile. He looked so irresistibly pleasant, in a word, that three or four good-humoured fellows said, "Good morning, sir! A merry Christmas to you!" And Scrooge said often afterwards, that of all the blithe sounds he had ever heard, those were the blithest in his ears.

He had not gone far, when coming on towards him he beheld the portly gentleman, who had walked into his counting-house the day before, and said, "Scrooge and Marley's, I believe?" It sent a pang across his heart to think how this old gentleman would look upon him when they met; but he knew what path lay straight before him, and he took it.

"My dear sir," said Scrooge, quickening his pace, and taking the old gentleman by both his hands. "How do you do? I hope you succeeded yesterday. It was very kind of you. A merry Christmas to you, sir!"

"Mr. Scrooge?"

"Yes," said Scrooge. "That is my name, and I fear it may not be pleasant to you. Allow me to ask your pardon. And will you have the goodness"—here Scrooge whispered in his ear.

"Lord bless me!" cried the gentleman, as if his breath were taken away. "My dear Mr. Scrooge, are you serious?"

"If you please," said Scrooge. "Not a farthing less. A great many back-payments are included in it, I assure you. Will you do me that favour?"

"My dear sir," said the other, shaking hands with him. "I don't know what to say to such munifi—"

"Don't say anything, please," retorted Scrooge. "Come and see me. Will you come and see me?"

"I will!" cried the old gentleman. And it was clear he meant to do it.

"Thank'ee," said Scrooge. "I am much obliged to you. I thank you fifty times. Bless you!"

He went to church, and walked about the streets, and watched the people hurrying to and fro, and patted children on the head, and questioned beggars, and looked down into the kitchens of houses, and up to the windows, and found that everything could yield him pleasure. He had never dreamed that any walk—that anything—could give him so much happiness. In the afternoon he turned his steps towards his nephew's house.

He passed the door a dozen times, before he had the courage to go up and knock. But he made a dash, and did it:

"Is your master at home, my dear?" said Scrooge to the girl. Nice girl! Very.

"Yes, sir."

"Where is he, my love?" said Scrooge.

"He's in the dining-room, sir, along with mistress. I'll show you up-stairs, if you please."

"Thank'ee. He knows me," said Scrooge, with his hand already on the dining-room lock. "I'll go in here, my dear."

He turned it gently, and sidled his face in, round the door. They were looking at the table (which was spread out in great array); for these young housekeepers are always nervous on such points, and like to see that everything is right.

"Fred!" said Scrooge.

Dear heart alive, how his niece by marriage started! Scrooge had forgotten, for the moment, about her sitting in the corner with the footstool, or he wouldn't have done it, on any account.

"Why bless my soul!" cried Fred, "who's that?"

"It's I. Your uncle Scrooge. I have come to dinner. Will you let me in, Fred?"

Let him in! It is a mercy he didn't shake his arm off. He was at home in five minutes. Nothing could be heartier. His niece looked just the same. So did Topper when he came. So did the plump sister when she came. So did every one when they came. Wonderful party, wonderful games, wonderful unanimity, won-der-ful happiness!

But he was early at the office next morning. Oh, he was early there. If he could only be there first, and catch Bob Cratchit coming late! That was the thing he had set his heart upon.

And he did it; yes, he did! The clock struck nine. No Bob. A quarter past. No Bob. He was full eighteen minutes and a half behind his time. Scrooge sat with his door wide open, that he might see him come into the Tank.

His hat was off, before he opened the door; his comforter too. He was on his stool in a jiffy; driving away with his pen, as if he were trying to overtake nine o'clock.

"Hallo!" growled Scrooge, in his accustomed voice, as near as he could feign it. "What do you mean by coming here at this time of day?"

"I am very sorry, sir," said Bob. "I am behind my time."

"You are?" repeated Scrooge. "Yes. I think you are. Step this way, sir, if you please."

"It's only once a year, sir," pleaded Bob, appearing from the Tank. "It shall not be repeated. I was making rather merry yesterday, sir."

"Now, I'll tell you what, my friend," said Scrooge, "I am not going to stand this sort of thing any longer. And therefore," he continued, leaping from his stool, and giving Bob such a dig in the waistcoat that he staggered back into the Tank again; "and therefore I am about to raise your salary!"

Bob trembled, and got a little nearer to the ruler. He had a momentary idea of knocking Scrooge down with it, holding him, and calling to the people in the court for help and a strait-waistcoat.

"A merry Christmas, Bob!" said Scrooge, with an earnestness that could not be mistaken, as he clapped him on the back. "A merrier Christmas, Bob, my good fellow, than I have given you, for many a year! I'll raise your salary, and endeavour to assist your struggling family, and we will discuss your affairs this very afternoon, over a Christmas bowl of smoking bishop, Bob! Make up the fires, and buy another coal-scuttle before you dot another i, Bob Cratchit!"

Scrooge was better than his word. He did it all, and infinitely more; and to Tiny Tim, who did NOT die, he was a second father. He became as good a friend, as good a master, and as good a man, as the good old city knew, or any other good old city, town, or borough, in the good old world. Some people laughed to see the alteration in him, but he let them laugh, and little heeded them; for he was wise enough to know that nothing ever happened on this globe, for good, at which some people did not have their fill of laughter in the outset; and knowing that such as these would be blind anyway, he thought it quite as well that they should wrinkle up their eyes in grins, as have the malady in less attractive forms. His own heart laughed: and that was quite enough for him.

He had no further intercourse with Spirits, but lived upon the Total Abstinence Principle, ever afterwards; and it was always said of him, that he knew how to keep Christmas well, if any man alive possessed the knowledge. May that be truly said of us, and all of us! And so, as Tiny Tim observed, God bless Us, Every One!

國家圖書館出版品預行編目資料

小氣財神（中英雙語典藏版）/ 查爾斯·狄更斯（Charles
Dickens）著；亞瑟·拉克姆（Arthur Rackham）、彭煥群繪；
辛一立譯. -- 二版. -- 臺中市：晨星，2023.06
　　面；　公分. --（愛藏本；118）
中英雙語典藏版
譯自：A Christmas Carol
ISBN 978-626-320-480-5（精裝）

873.596　　　　　　　　　　　　　　　　112007409

愛藏本：118

小氣財神（中英雙語典藏版）
A Christmas Carol

作　　者｜查爾斯·狄更斯（Charles Dickens）
繪　　者｜亞瑟·拉克姆（Arthur Rackham）、彭煥群
譯　　者｜辛一立

執行編輯｜江品如
封面設計｜鐘文君
美術編輯｜黃偵瑜
文字校潤｜呂昀慶、江品如

創 辦 人｜陳銘民
發 行 所｜晨星出版有限公司
　　　　　407 台中市西屯區工業 30 路 1 號 1 樓
　　　　　TEL：04-23595820　FAX：04-23550581
　　　　　https://star.morningstar.com.tw
　　　　　行政院新聞局版台業字第 2500 號
法律顧問｜陳思成律師

讀者專線｜TEL：02-23672044 / 04-2359-5819#212
傳真專線｜FAX：02-23635741 / 04-23595493
讀者信箱｜service@morningstar.com.tw
網路書店｜https://www.morningstar.com.tw
郵政劃撥｜15060393　知己圖書股份有限公司

初版日期｜2002 年 10 月 31 日
二版日期｜2023 年 06 月 15 日
　ISBN｜978-626-320-480-5
　定價｜新台幣 310 元

印　　刷｜上好印刷股份有限公司

填寫線上回函，立刻享有
晨星網路書店50元購書金